C000285605

A Night in a
Moorish Harem

THE SCARLET LIBRARY
LONDON MMI

THE SCARLET LIBRARY
is an imprint of
THE *Erotic* Print Society ®
EPS, 1 Maddox Street
LONDON W1S 2PZ

Tel (UK only): 0800 026 25 24
Fax: +44 (0)20 7437 3528
Email: *eros@eps.org.uk*
Web: *www.scarletlibrary.com*
OR *www.eroticprints.org*

ISBN: 1-898998-39-6

© 2001 MacHo Ltd, London UK

No part of this publication may be reproduced by any means
without the express written permission of the Publishers. The moral
right of the author of the designated drawings has been asserted.

A Night in a Moorish Harem

ANONYMOUS

with new
illustrations by

HARRY
DOUGLAS

THE SCARLET LIBRARY

CONTENTS

FOREWORD

THE BOOK

The first appearance of *A Night in a Moorish Harem* was in Paris in the late 1890's. Redolent with orientalist mystery and exoticism, its antecedent can be found in a much earlier novel, *The Lustful Turk* of 1828, a tale of youthful English maidenhood being ravished by the eponymous Ottoman. But the actions of the *Moorish Harem's* hero, Lord George Herbert, are in direct antithesis to the 'stiff insertions' and 'horrid practises' visited upon the (often willing) victims of the randy Bey. For here is the Empire striking back with the confident swagger of an aristocratic young Englishman, indeed, a dashing Royal Navy Captain (at the rather surprising age of twenty-three), who loves a plump thigh as much as he does a slender one, and who is determined to show these Mediterranean girls how passionate, virile and enduring a Briton can be.

THE ARTIST

Harry Douglas has illustrated half a dozen books during his career as a landscape painter. Trained at the Royal Academy Schools, his fine-art and illustrational work possess a vibrancy of colour that is as distinctive as his highly original sense of composition. Douglas, a keen traveller, often finds inspiration for his work in the Mediterranean countries that he visits.

PREFACE

Lord George Herbert is universally acknowledged to be the handsomest man in English nobility. His form is tall and muscular, but of a perfect symmetry. His features are handsome, but manly, and of a ruddy bronze colour, acquired at sea.

His short and curly brown hair shades a broad and white forehead, beneath which sparkle large blue eyes. He wars a heavy beard and moustache, but they are not able to conceal his handsome mouth.

His courage and talent, together with the influence of his family, had procured for him at the early age of twenty-three the command of one of the finest ships in the English navy. The following strange but true narrative is from his pen, and it may be imagined that he did not intend to have it copied.

But he left it in the possession of a fair and frail lady who thought it too good to keep secret, and so the reader has the benefit of it.

ABDALLAH PASHA'S SERAGLIO

Her British Majesty's ship *Antler*, of which I was in command, lay becalmed one afternoon off the coast of Morocco. I did not allow the steam to be raised, for I knew the evening breeze would soon make toward the land. Retiring to my cabin, I threw myself upon the sofa. I could not sleep, for my thoughts kept wandering back to the beautiful women of London, and the favours which some of them had granted me when last on shore. Months had gone since then and months more would elapse before I could again hope to quench, in the laps of beauty, the hot desire which now coursed through my veins and distended my genitals. To divert my mind from thoughts at present so unprofitable, I resolved to take a bath.

Beneath the stern windows which lighted my cabin lay a small boat, into which I got by sliding down a rope which held it to the ship. Then I undressed and plunged into the cool waves. After bathing, I dressed and, reclining in the boat, fell asleep.

When I awoke it was dark and I was floating alone near the shore with the ship miles away. The rope which held the boat must have slipped when the breeze sprung up, and the people on the ship, being busy getting under way, had not noticed me.

I had no oars and dared not use the sail for fear the

Moorish vessels in sight would discover me. I drifted toward a large building which was the only one to be seen; it rose from the water's edge. The approach to the place on which it stood seemed to be from the land side, and all the windows which I could see were high above the ground. The keel of my boat soon grated on the sand and I hastened to pull it among the rocks for concealment, or it was quite possible I might be seized and sold into slavery if discovered; my plan was to wait for the land breeze just before dawn and escape to sea.

At this moment I heard a whispered call from above. I looked up and saw two ladies looking down at me from one of the windows, and behind them were gathered several others whom I could just see in the gloom. 'We have been watching you,' said one of the ladies, 'and will try to assist you; wait where you are.' She spoke French, which is the common medium of communication among the different nations inhabiting the shores of the Mediterranean, and which had become familiar to me. I now thought this isolated building was a seraglio, and I resolved to trust the ladies who ran even more risk than myself in case of discovery. After waiting some time a rope of shawls was let down from the window and the same voice bade me climb. The discipline of my training when a midshipman made this easy for me to do.

I rose hand over hand and safely reached the window, through which I was assisted by the ladies into the perfumed air of an elegant apartment, richly furnished and brilliantly lighted. My first duty was to kiss the hands which had aided me, and then I explained the accident which brought me among them and the plan which I had formed for escape before dawn. I then gave them my name and rank.

While doing this, I had an opportunity to observe the ladies. There were nine of them, and any one of them would have been remarked for her beauty anywhere. Each one of them differed from all the others in the style of her charms. Some were large and some were small, some slender and some plump, some blonde and some brunette; but all were bewitchingly beautiful. Each, too, was the most lovely type of a different nationality; for war and shipwrecks and piracy enable the Moorish Pashas to choose their darlings from all the flags that float on the Mediterranean. A lady whom they called Inez, and whom, therefore, I took to be a Spaniard, answered me by bidding me in the name of all of them the warmest welcome. 'You are,' she said, 'in the seraglio of Abdallah, Pasha of the district, who is not expected until tomorrow, and who will never be the wiser if his ladies seize the opportunity to entertain a gentleman during his absence.

'We have no secrets of jealousies among ourselves,' she said, smiling very significantly.

'That is most unusual,' I remarked. 'How can any of you know whether she has any secrets with the one he happens to be alone with?'

'But none of us are ever alone with him,' replied Inez. The blank look of consternation I wore set them all to laughing. They were brimful of mischief, and evidently bent on making the most of the unexpected company of a young man. Inez put her hand on my sleeve. 'How wet your are,' said she. 'It would not be hospitable to allow you to keep on such wet clothes.' My clothes were perfectly dry, but the winks and smiles which the young ladies exchanged as they began to disrobe me led me to submit cheerfully while they proceeded to divest me of every article of clothing. When at length my shirt was suddenly jerked off they gave little screams and peeped through their fingers at my shaft, which by this time was of most towering dimensions.

I had snatched a hearty kiss from one and all of them as they had gathered round to undress me.

Inez now handed me a scarf which she had taken from her own fair shoulders. 'We can none of us bear to leave you,' she said, 'but you can only kiss one at a time; please throw this to the lady you prefer.' Good heavens! Then it was true that all of these beautiful ladies had been accustomed to be present when one of them was embraced.

'Ladies,' said I, 'you are unfair; you have stripped me, but you leave those charms concealed which you offer my preference. I am sure none of you have any imperfections which you wish to keep covered.' The ladies looked at one another, blushed a little, nodded and laughed, and then began undressing. Velvet vests, skirts of lawn and silken trousers were rapidly flung to the floor; lastly, as if it were a given signal, every dainty chemise was stripped off, and nine of the most lovely forms that ever floated throughout a sculptor's dream stood naked before me. Was I dreaming, or had I suddenly been transported to the seventh heaven?

For a while I stood entranced, gazing at the charming spectacle. 'Ladies,' said I, 'at least it would be immodest in me to give preference when all are so ravishingly lovely. Please keep the scarf, fair Inez – and when I have paid a tribute to your fair charms pass it yourself to another – until all have been gratified.'

'Did he say all?' asked a little brunette.

'All indeed!' cried the rest in chorus bursting into laughter. 'Everyone,' said I, 'or I will perish in the attempt.' Inez was standing directly in front of me.

She was about nineteen and of that rarest type of Spanish beauty, partly derived from Elanders Hood.

Her eyes were sparkling brown, but her long hair was blonde. It was braided and coiled around the top of her head like a crown, which added to her queenly appearance for she was of normal stature; her plump and well-rounded form harmonised with her height. Her complexion had the slight yellow tinge of rich cream, which was set off by the rosy nipples that tipped her full breasts and the still deeper hue of her lips and mouth. She happened to be standing on one of the silken cushions which singly and in piles lay scattered about the room in profusion. It made her height just equal to my own. As soon as I had made the speech last recorded, I advanced and folded her in my embrace. Her soft arms were wound around me in response, and our lips met in a delicious and prolonged kiss, during which my shaft was imprisoned against her warm smooth belly. Then she raised herself on tiptoe, which brought its crest among the short thick hair where the belly terminated. With one hand I guided my shaft to the entrance, which welcomed it; with my other I held her plump buttocks toward me.

Then she gradually settled on her feet again, and as she did so the entrance to her moist, hot and swollen sheath was slowly and delightfully brought about.

When she was on her feet again, I could feel her throbbing womb resting on my shaft.

The other ladies gathered around us, their kisses rained on my neck and shoulders, and the pressure of their bosoms was against my back and sides; indeed, they so completely sustained Inez and myself that I seemed about to mingle my being with them all at once. I had stirred the being of Inez with but a few thrusts when the rosy cheeks took on a deeper dye, her eyes swam, her lips parted and I felt a delicious baptism of moisture on my shaft.

Then her head sank on my shoulder and the gathered sperm of months gushed from my crest so profusely that I seemed completely transferred with the waves of rapture into the beautiful Spanish girl.

Her sighs of pleasure were not only echoed by mine, but by all the ladies in sympathy gathered around us. They gently lowered us from their sustaining embrace to a pile of cushions. As they did so with hardly any aid on our part, my diminished shaft was drawn out of Inez and with some of my tributary sperm, which splashed on the floor.

'It was bad of you, Inez, to take more than you could keep,' said one of the others. She said it in such a pitiful tone it convulsed us all with laughter.

As for me, I now realised the rashness of the promise I had made them all. They gaily joined hands around Inez and myself and began a circling dance.

Their round, white limbs and plump bosoms floated in the lamp-light as they moved in cadence to a Moorish love song in which they all joined.

With my cheeks pillowed against the soft, full breasts of Inez, I watched the charming circle, which was like a scene from fairyland. Bracelets and anklets of heavy gold gleamed on their arms and legs; rings, necklaces and earrings of diamonds and rubies, which they had in profusion, glittered at every moment. Each one had her hair elaborately dressed in the style most becoming to her, and there were no envious garments to conceal a single charm. I urged them to prolong the bewitching spectacle again and again, which they obligingly did. Then they gathered around me, reclining to rest on the cushion as near as they could get in attitudes which were picturesque and voluptuous.

While we were thus resting I frequently exchanged a kiss or caress with my fair companions, which I took care to do impartially. Then it occurred to me that I would like to hear from the lips of each the most interesting and voluptuous passage from their lives. Again these interesting ladies, after a little urging, consented to my wishes. Inez commenced.

THE SPANISH LADY'S STORY

'We lived in Seville. When at the age of sixteen my parents promised me in marriage to a gentleman whom I had seen but twice and did not admire. My love was already given to Carlos, a handsome young officer who had just been promoted for his bravery. He was elegantly formed; his hair and eyes were as dark as night, and he could dance to perfection. But it was for his gentle, winning smile that I loved him. On the evening of the day my parents had announced their determination to me, I had gone to be alone in the orange grove in the farthest part of our garden, there to sorrow over my hard fate.

In the midst of my grief I heard the voice of Carlos calling me. Could it be he who had been banished from the house and whom I never expected to see again? He sprang down from the garden wall, folded me in his embrace and covered my hair with kisses, for I had hidden my blushing face on his bosom. Then we talked of our sad lot. Carlos was poor and it would be impossible to marry without the consent of my parents. We could only mingle our tears and regrets. He led me to a grassy bank concealed by orange trees and rose bushes. Then he drew me on his lap and kissed my lips and cheeks and eyes. I did not chide him, for it must be our last meeting, but I did not return his kisses with passion, I had never felt a wanton desire in my life, much less when I was so sad. His passionate kisses were no longer confined to my face, but were showered on my neck, and at length my dress was parted and revealed my little bosoms to his ardent lips. I was startled and made an attempt to stop him in what I considered an impropriety, but he did not stop there. I felt my skirts raised, and a mingled sensation of alarm and shame accused me to try to prevent it, but it was impossible. I loved him too much to struggle long against him, and he was soon lying between my naked thighs. "Inez," he said, "If you love me be my wife these few minutes before we part." I could not resist the appeal.

'I offered my lips to his kisses without any feeling save innocent love, and lay passive, while I felt him guide a stiff, warm object between my thighs. It entered where nothing had ever gone before, and no sooner had it done so than he gave me a fierce thrust which seemed to tear my vitals with a cruel pain; then he gave a deep sigh and sank heavily on my bosom. I kissed him repeatedly for I supposed it had hurt him just as much as it had me, little thinking that his pleasure was as exquisite as my suffering.

'Just at that moment the harsh voice of my duenna resounded through the garden, calling, "Inez! Inez!"

'Exchanging with my seducer a lingering, hearty kiss, I extracted myself from his embrace and answered the call. My duenna eyed me sharply as I approached her. "Why do you straddle your legs so far apart when you walk?" she asked as I came closer. "Why is the bosom of your dress so disordered, and why are your cheeks so flushed?" I made some excuse about climbing to get an orange and hurried to my room. I locked the door and prepared to go to bed, that I might think uninterruptedly of Carlos, whom I now loved more than ever. When I took off my petticoat I found it all stained with blood.

'I folded it up and placed it beneath my pillow to dream upon, under the fond delusion that Carlos' blood was mingled with my own. For a few weeks afterwards I was so closely watched that I could not see Carlos. On the evening preceding my marriage I went to vespers with my duenna. While we were kneeling in the cathedral a large woman, closely veiled, came and knelt beside me. She attracted my attention by pulling my dress. As I turned to her, she momentarily lifted the corner of mantilla, and I saw it was Carlos in disguise. I was not on the alert, and a small package was slipped into my hand. I had just time to conceal it in my bosom when my duenna arose and we left the church. As soon as I regained the privacy of my room I tore open the package and found in contained a silken rope-ladder and a letter from Carlos requesting me to suspend it from my window that night after the family was at rest. The note was full of love.

'There was much more to tell, it said, if I would grant the interview by means of the ladder. Of course I determined to see him. I was ignorant of what most girls learn from each other, for I had no companion. I supposed when a woman was embraced as I had been, she necessarily got with child, and that such embraces therefore occurred at intervals of a year or so. I expected consequently nothing of the kind at the coming interview. I wanted to learn of Carlos if the child I supposed to be in my womb would be born so soon as to betray our secret to my husband. When the family retired I went to my room and dressed myself elaborately, braiding my hair and putting on all of my jewellery.

'I then fastened one end of the rope-ladder to the bedpost and lowered the other end out of the window. It was at once strained by the ascending step of Carlos. My eyes were soon feasted with the sight of my lover, and then we were locked in each other's arms. Again and again we alternately devoured each other with our eyes and pressed each other to our hearts. Words did not seem to be of any use; our kisses and caresses became more passionate and for the first time in my life I felt a wanton emotion. The lips between my thighs became moistened and torrid with coursing blood; I could feel my cheeks burn under the ardent gaze of my lover; I could no longer meet his eyes; my own dropped in shame. He began to undress me rapidly, his hands trembled with eagerness. Could it be, he wanted to pierce my loins so soon again, as he had done in the orange garden? An hour ago I would have dreaded; now the thought caused throbs of welcome just where the pain had been sharpest. Stripped to my chemise, and even that unbuttoned by the eager hand of my lover, I darted from his arms and concealed my confusion beneath the covers.

'He soon undressed and followed me; one kiss on my cheeks and one on each of my naked bosoms, then he opened my thighs and parted the little curls between. Again I felt the stiff, warm object entering; it went in slowly on account of the tightness, but every inch of its progress inward became more and more pleasant. When it had fully entered I was in a rapture of delight, yet something was wanting. I dropped my arms around my lover and responded passionately to his kisses. I was almost tempted to respond to his thrusts by a wanton motion of my loins. My maiden-head was gone and the tender virgin wound completely healed, but I still had a remnant of maidenly shame. For a moment he lay still and then he gave me half a dozen deep thrusts, each one giving me more and more pleasure, it culminated at last in a thrill so exquisite that my frame seemed to melt; nothing more was wanting! I gave a sigh of deep gratification and my arms fell helpless to my sides! But I received with passionate pleasure two or three more thrusts, which Carlos gave me. At each of them my sheath was penetrated by a copious gush that soothed and bathed its heated membranes.

'For a long time we lay perfectly still; the stiff shaft, which had completely filled me, had diminished in size until it seemed entirely out. Carlos at last relieved me of his weight by lying by my side, but our legs were still entwined. We now had time to converse; my lover explained to me all the sexual mysteries, which remained for me to know. Then we formed plans which after marriage would enable us to meet often. These explanations and plans were mingled so freely with caresses that before my lover had left me we had melted five times in each other's arms. I had barely strength to draw up the rope-ladder after he had departed. The day had now begun to dawn and I fell into a dreamless sleep, being awakened by my duenna pounding on the door and calling that it was nearly 10 o'clock, and that I was to be married at 11. I was in no hurry, but they got me to church in time; during the whole ceremony I felt my lover's sperm trickling down my thighs.'

We all applauded as she thus finished her story. While she was telling her story, one of the ladies, whom I had noticed to be the most fleshy of the number cuddled up close to my side and suffered me to explore all of her charms with my hand. During the description of the scene in the orange garden my fingers toyed with the curls between her thighs, and as the story went on, I parted the curls and felt the lips beneath. She was partly on her belly against me, so that this by-play was not observed; my fingers were encouraged by the lady's hand until two of them made an entrance and were completely enclosed in the hot, moist tissue.

The little protuberance all women have within the orifice, and which is the principal seat of sensation, was in her remarkably developed. It was as large as the end of my little finger. I played with it and squeezed it and plunged my two fingers past it again and again. She manifested her delight by kissing me on the neck where she had hidden her face.

When Inez described her first thrill in the bedroom scene, my fingers were doing all in their power to complete the other lady's gratification, and this, too, with success, for they were suddenly bathed with moisture and the lady drew a deep sigh, which was not noticed, for all supposed it to be in sympathy with Inez's story. Then she withdrew my hand and lay perfectly still. Inez was about to give her her scarf, but she lay so motionless that she handed it to another. 'This,' said Inez, 'is Helene, a Grecian lady; she will tell you a story and then she will do anything you wish.' My head was still pillowed on Inez's breast. Helene smiled and then stooped and kissed me. She was about medium height; very slender, but graceful and well-rounded, and her skin was alabaster. Her features were of the perfect antique mould and were lighted with fine grey eyes. Her glossy black hair was all brushed back to a knot just below the back of her neck, from which but a single curl escaped on either side and toyed with her firm and finely rounded bosoms.

The deep vermilion of her lips compensated for the faint colour of her cheeks, whose tinge was scarcely deeper than that of the hard little nipples that tipped her bosoms or that of her small and finely-cut ears. She was about twenty-two, and ripe to yield. I drew her down to a seat on my loins and begged her to begin her story.

THE GRECIAN LADY'S STORY

'I entered the bridal bed a virgin. When the bridesmaids left me I trembled with apprehension and covered up my head in the bed clothing; it was because I had heard so many stories of the trials and hardships of a virgin on her wedding night and not because I had any antipathy for my husband; on the contrary, I liked him. His courtship had been short, for he was a busy man in diplomatic service of the Greek government. He was no longer young, but he was good-looking and manly, and I was proud that he had selected me from the other Athenian girls. He came to the side of my bed, and turning down the clothes from my head he saw how I was agitated. My heart beat still more violently when he entered. He simply kissed my hand and then went to the other side of the room to undress; this conduct somewhat reassured me. When he got into bed and took me n his arms my back was turned toward him. He took no liberties with any part of my person, but began to converse with me about the incidents of the wedding. I was soon so calm that I suffered him to turn me with my face toward him and kiss me first on the forehead and then on the lips. After a while he begged me to return his kisses, saying that if I did not it would prove that I disliked him. Thus encouraged, I returned his kisses.

'When I had been so long in his arms that I began to feel at home, he turned me upon my back, unfastened the bosom of my chemise, and kissed and fondled my breasts. This set my heart to beating wildly again, but I kept exchanging kisses till he suddenly lifted the skirt of my chemise and lay between my thighs. Then I covered my face with my hands for shame, but he was so kind and gentle I soon got accustomed to the situation and I suffered him to remove my hands and fasten his mouth to mine in a passionate kiss; as he did so I felt something pushing between my thighs. It entered amid the curls and touched the naked lips beneath.

'I felt my face grow hot with shame and I lay perfectly passive. He must have been in bed with me two hours before he ventured so far. He had his reward, for a soft desire began to grow in my brain; the blood centred in my loins and I longed for the connection which was so imminent. I returned him a kiss as passionate as he gave; it was the signal for which he had been waiting. I felt a pressure on the virgin membrane, not hard enough however to be painful. The pressure slackened and then pushed again and again. By this time I was wanton with desire, and not only returned the passionate kisses, but wound my arms around him. Then came that fatal thrust, tearing away the obstruction and reaching to the very depths of my loins. I gave a cry of mingled bliss and agony, which I could not help repeating at each of three deep thrusts that followed. Then all was still and an effusion-like balm filled my sheath in place of the organ that had so disturbed it. A delightful languor stole over my frame and I went to sleep in my husband's arms.

'In less than six months circumstances compelled me to deceive him. After we had been married a while our position required us to go a great deal in company. Card playing was very fashionable and the stakes got very high. One night the luck was terribly against me. I proposed for the party to double. My husband had gone on a journey a few days before and had left a large sum of money in my charge; it was nearly all his fortune. A portion of this money I now staked, thinking that the luck could not possibly go against me again. But it did.

'I was rendered desperate; again I proposed to double, it would take all I had left if I lost. The ladies who were playing withdrew; the gentlemen were too polite to do so. The cards were against me; I felt myself grow deadly pale. The French ambassador, Count Henri, who was sitting beside me, was disposed to conceal my terrible embarrassment; he was very stalwart. His manners were very engaging; he kept up a stream of small talk till the others had dispersed to other parts of the room; then he offered to bring me on the morrow the amount I had lost. I turned crimson as I had before been pale; I knew too well the price of such assistance. I made him no reply. My eyes dropped to the floor and I begged him to leave me, which he politely did.

All the next day I was nearly distracted. I hoped Count Henri would not come, my cheeks would burn as on the evening before, and the blood all rushed back to my heart. At three o'clock he came, the valet showed him to the parlour, closed the door and retired. Count Henri must have known he was expected, for I was elegantly dressed in blue silk and my shoulders were set off with heavy lace; I was so agitated I could not rise from the sofa to greet him.

"'May I have the happiness of being your confidant?" he asked, as he seated himself beside me, holing in one hand a well-filled purse and dropping the other about my waist. I could not reject the purse; if I kept it I could not ask him to remove his arm; I was giddy with contending emotions.

"'For God's sake spare me!" I murmured. My head drooped and he pressed it to his heart; I fainted away. When I became conscious I was lying on my back upon the sofa, in the arms of the Count, the lace at my bosom was parted, my heavy skirts all turned up from my naked thighs, and he was in the very ecstasy of filling my sheath with sperm. It was this exquisite sensation which restored me to consciousness, but it became limber and small, and I was left hopelessly in the lurch. Then I beseeched him to go; it was no time or place for this. "Will you receive me in your bedroom tonight?" asked he, kissing my bare bosoms. He had so excited my passions that I no longer hesitated. "The front door will be unfastened all night," I replied, "and my room is directly over this one." Then he allowed me to rise; I adjusted my distorted dress as quickly as possible, but it was not quick enough; the valet opened the door to bring the card of a visitor; he saw enough to put me in his power. When the Count had gone I found the purse in my bosom; it contained more than I had lost, but my thoughts were not of money; my lips had tasted the forbidden fruit. I was no longer the same woman, my excitement had culminated in lascivious desire, I could hardly wait for night to come.

'When finally the house was still, I unfastened the front door, retired to my room, undressed and was standing in my chemise, with my night-gown in my hand ready to put on, when the door of my room opened and Alex, the valet, stood before me with a finger on his lips. He was a fine looking youth of seventeen. A Hungarian of a reduced family, who acted half in the capacity of secretary and half in that of valet for my husband. I could not help giving a faint scream, while I concealed my person as much as possible with the night-gown.

'"My lady," said he, "I know all. But I shall be discreet; I only ask you to give me the sweetest proof of your confidence." There was no help for it; with a murmur for shame I sprang into bed and hid under the bed clothes; he quickly undressed and followed; my object was to dismiss him before the Count came. I therefore suffered him to made rapid progress. He took me in his arms and kissed my lips and bosoms, and as he raised my chemise our naked thighs met. He was more agitated than myself; I had been anticipating a paramour all afternoon, while he could not have known what reception would be accorded him; he could hardly guide his shaft to the lips that welcomed it; as for myself, I

began where I had left off with the Count, my sheath with wanton greediness devoured every inch that entered it, and at the very first thrust I melted with an adulterous rapture never felt in my husband's embrace.

'Just at that moment I heard the front door softly open and shut. I pushed Alex away with a force that drew his stiff shaft completely out of me.

'"Gather up your clothes quickly and get into the closet," I said. Madly eager as he must have been to finish, he hurried with his clothes into the closet, the door of which just shut as the Count entered.

'The Count came up and kissed me, I pretended to be asleep; he undressed hastily, got into bed and took me in his arms. But I delayed his progress as much as possible; I made him tell me everything that had been said about my losses at cards; I used every artifice to keep him at bay until his efforts should arouse my passions; then he mounted me; his stalwart shaft distended and penetrated me so much deeper than that of young Alex that it was more exquisite than before. Again the wild, adulterous thrill penetrated every part of my body. Suddenly, I cried, "Under the bed with you!" He pulled his stiff shaft out of me with a curse of disappointment that he could not finish, and scrambled under the bed, dragging his clothes with him. My husband came in all beaming with delight that he had been able to return so soon.

'I received him with much demonstration. "How it flushes your cheeks to see me," he said. When he undressed and came to bed I returned his caresses with

so much ardour that he soon entered where Alex and
the Count had so hastily with drawn. It was pleasant,
but I feigned much more rapture that I felt. To console
the Count I dropped one of my hands down alongside of
the bed and he was so polite as to kiss it; as my
husband's face was buried in my neck, and he was
making rapid thrusts, I kissed my other hand to Alex,
who was peering out of the closet. Then I gave motion
to my loins, which sent my husband spending, and
repeated it till I had extracted from him the most
copious gushes; it was too soon for me to melt with
another thrill; my object was to fix him for a sound
sleep, but the balmy sperm was so grateful to my sheath
after the two fierce preceding encounters that I felt
rewarded for my troubles. He soon fell asleep. I then
motioned for the Count to go. With his clothes in one
hand and his stiff shaft in the other he glided out. Soon
after I heard the front door shut, and the disconsolate
Alex came forth, his clothes under his arm and both
hands holding his rigid staff; he, too, disappeared.' Here
Helene finished.

During her story I lay on my back, resting on Inez's
bosom. Helene set astride of my loins with her face
toward me, which gave me a fair view of her most secret
beauties. She had carelessly let the scarf fall over our
laps, and under its protecting cover her little tapering
fingers began to play with my limber shaft. As the story
proceeded it began to stiffen, and as she was describing
the bedchamber scene she contrived to slip it into the

crevice so directly above it. It rose until it was almost rigid, vivified as it was by the close retreat in which it was hidden. She kept undulating her loins as the story went on until, just as she finished, I was nearly ready; at the same moment I felt my shaft moistened by the libation of the Greek girl, and she fell fainting into the arms of a lady close by. My shaft drew out of her with a sucking noise that set all to laughing. She hurriedly gave the scarf to the lady in whose arms she lay and in whose bosom she had her face. 'It is with you, Zuleika,' they all cried in chorus. Zuleika looked very much embarrassed.

About eighteen years of age, she was formed very much like Inez, whom she equalled in height, but she was more muscular, and her skin was of deep bronze.

Her large, lustrous eyes were dark as night; as was her curly hair, which was set off by a snowy turban, on which gleamed a crescent of burnished silver. The colour deepened in her dusky cheeks as she drew close to me and timidly began her story.

THE MOORISH LADY'S STORY

'Ladies, she said, you all know I am three months gone with child; you have now to learn what is equally true; I am still a virgin.'

'A virgin and with child!' they all echoed, several of them crossing themselves as they exclaimed.

'Listen and you shall hear,' proceeded Zuleika.

'I was purchased from my parents in Fez, where we lived, by a young Moorish merchant. They, as well as myself, were delighted at the prospects which he promised, to transfer me to the harem of some great Moorish Pasha. The price paid was very high as I was warranted a virgin. The next morning we joined the caravan for Morocco. Mounted on my camel, I enjoyed the trip in the highest spirits. Ali, my master, rode beside me on a fine horse which he managed with grace and vigour. His person was slender, and his features, which were at the same time bold and amiable, captured my fancy. His attentions to me were unremitting; his tent every night was pitched near my own to guard me from intrusion. The last night on the road I had retired early and was just sinking to sleep as the darkness fell, when Ali appeared in my tent.

'"What is your will, my lord?" I asked. He knelt down and kissed me; it was the first time he had done so.

'"My wish is to make you my wife," he replied. "And why should you not, my lord?" I asked again. Then he told me all his fortune was invested in my purchase, and that it would only bring poverty and misery on us both. We mingled our regrets and caresses, which now grew more and more ardent, until I found myself lying beneath him with my bosoms bared to his kisses and my naked thighs parted. Beneath them I felt a gentle pressure which penetrated the hair and touched the sensitive lips again.

'I lay passive with my eyes shut. A soft desire ran through my frame, and centring at the lips where Ali was pressing, and making the pressure delightful.

'The longer he continued in this position the more I wished for a deeper and more gratifying thrust.

'But the gentle pushes he gave barely parted the outside lips. I could feel that they were stopped by the virgin membrane that barred all further entrance. I grew with desire; I strained him to my bosom, and pressing my mouth to his, I was relieved of a melting thrill. At the same moment I felt Ali's answering throb and a gush of sperm penetrated to the depths of my loins, far within the still unbroken curtain of my virginity. For a long time we lay in a voluptuous but motionless repose. Then Ali tore himself away from my arms. "I must go," he said; "I could not resist another such temptation." It is three months since that sweet but imperfect connection, which is now certain will result in my being a mother.'

'And has no man touched you since?' I asked, with the deeper interest, as I took the splendid Moorish girl in my arms.

'I can tell you,' said Inez, 'why the Pasha, who never before suffered a woman to remain a virgin a single night in his harem, has spared her. He purchased her from Ali on the day she arrived from Morocco. After having her examined by the old woman in his employ, she was brought here, and the same evening, as soon as he had finished his supper, he threw his handkerchief to her. She retired to receive him in her room alone, as only a virgin in this harem has the privilege of doing.

'For, as you already know, it is customary for us to receive the Pasha's embraces when we are all present. I noticed Zuleika looked very reluctant; she was no doubt thinking of Ali, from whom she had so recently parted. I overtook her at the door of the bridal chamber. "Let me take your place for tonight," said I; "we are of the same size, and complexions will not show in the dark; the Pasha shall never know."

'"Can you indeed manage it?" she asked; "if so you are welcome." Then she hurried away, and I entered the bridal chamber in her place, undressed, extinguished the light, and got into bed. Before a great while the Pasha came. He kissed me on the back of my neck, for I had buried my face in the pillow like a bashful girl. Then he hurriedly undressed, and stretching himself beside me, took me in his arms. My heart was beating violently for the success of my bold scheme. But this agitation he took for virgin fright. I answered in monosyllables to his questions, and shrank from every caress he bestowed on my bosom and thighs.

'He became, as I intended he should, only more eager. When at last he mounted me I covered my face with my hands as if in a paroxysm of shame, and wrapping one of my legs over the other I held them tightly together. He had to lie with his thighs parted over mine. In this position he guided his crest between them, worked its way among the hair and began to enter the tightly squeezed lips beneath.

'My passion had become so thoroughly aroused by this time that I could scarcely help opening my thighs and letting him have free entrance. My monthly period was just passing off, in the latter part of which a woman is peculiarly susceptible to desire. But I made him gain his way by the hardest pushing. Not only were my thighs locked but I concentrated the muscles of my sheath at the lips. He would give a fierce but ineffective thrust; then he would squeeze and suck my bosom; until at last my wantonness became uncontrollable and I gave way with a rapture that unnerved me as I let his shaft plunge in to the hilt. He spent profusely with a long sigh of triumphant satisfaction. I gave a sigh equally profound; I could not help it. But it only completed his delusion, for he thought it was caused by the pain I suffered at the loss of my maiden-head. He petted and consoled me with kisses and caresses until we were both ready for another embrace. This time he did not expect to encounter any resistance. He met with none, though I took care to be sufficiently coy at his embrace. Then he fell asleep. I know he would wake in the morning with a stiff shaft, so just before down, I went and took a bath, put on my most seductive apparel, adorned myself with musk. Soon I heard him call: "Zuleika! Zuleika!" I hastened to his bedside.

"'Zuleika begs that you will excuse her, my lord," said I; "pray have some mercy on the poor girl." Then I turned down the sheet and exposed the blood stains occasioned by my monthly period. 'See,' said I, 'you have butchered her.' Then you must come to bed," he replied.

'This was just what I sought, and I lost no time in doing so. For the third time I got all I wanted.'

As for me, I had been caressing Zuleika. Her plump bosoms, her smooth belly and her grand thighs passed in review under my hands. She concealed her face on my breast, but she made no resistance. Perhaps she no longer thought of Ali.

I even ventured to insert my forefinger between the lips which concealed her maiden-head. It stretched from side to side of her entire sheath, save for the little orifice which is never closed. She raised her face which was overspread with a crimson flush. Her eyes were closed, but her mouth pouted for the kiss which my lips at once fastened upon it.

The voluptuous stories and the wanton situation had done their work on her. My intrusive finger felt a throbbing of the lips between which it was inserted. My shaft had become rigid as a bone. The glands clung to its base ready for action. As soon as Inez finished speaking I laid Zuleika on her back upon the cushions, spread her thighs wide open and mounted her. My crest was at once buried where my fingers had lately explored. I gave a push that strained the virgin membrane, but it had the strength which characterised the rest of her splendid physique and bounded back like rubber. Her whole form quivered at the touch. Furious with lust, I wrapped my arms around the small of her back and braced my whole strength for another thrust.

My crest went plunging in, tore through the curtain of her virginity and rammed against her pregnant womb. 'Allah! Allah!' she moaned, tossing her arms wildly upward and rolling her eyes toward heaven. Whether her pain or her pleasure was most exquisite I do not know, but my whole being seemed to centre in my loins and gush into the beautiful Moor. Then I sank prostrate and exhausted on her bosom with every desire gratified.

'The baby has been fed,' said Inez, which caused another laugh among the ladies.

'See Zuleika,' said another, in an alarmed tone. 'She has fainted!' Zuleika had indeed become very pale. One gave her a glass of water and bather her forehead. Another took the scarf from her hand and staunched the blood that was flowing from her thighs. I supported her head on my arm and gave her kisses, which before long she began to return. Then she threw one leg over me to conceal the traces of her wound, saying to the lady who had been using the scarf that she bequeathed it to her. This lady's name was Laura, and she was an Italian. It was the same one who had melted at the

touch of my fingers during the first story.

She was about twenty-four years old and the most fleshy lady in the room. Her immense bosoms and buttocks quivered as she moved, but rounded out again in perfect contour when she was still.

She had dimples on her cheeks and chin, dimples at her elbows and knees, and dimples at her hips. Her features were very pleasing, with a rosy mouth, a saucy *retroussé* nose, and eyes that were dark in expression and shaded by long lashes. Her long hair was worn in puffs, supported by a tall comb, doubtless to add to her stature, which was only medium, notwithstanding her enormous weight. Still her waist was not overgrown, and her wrists and ankles were pretty. 'I think I shall have time to tell a long story,' she said, glancing at the diminished little object between my legs. Amid the titters caused by this remark, seating herself beside me, she began.

THE ITALIAN LADY'S STORY

'I am sorry to confess that I did not have a maiden-head when I was married. It was a jealousy and suspicion on my husband's mind which I could not eradicate. When I was a girl of sixteen, at a school in a convent, one of my companions handed me an improper book. It contained the amours of the ancient gods and goddesses. They were painted so minutely that nothing was left to be imagined, and it so fascinated me that I at once began it. I retired to my room and bolted my door to devour it undisturbed. I took off my clothes and, putting on my dressing gown, lay on my bed to read at ease. Alone as I was, my cheeks burned at the lascivious descriptions in the book. Then I longed to be in the place of one of the goddesses or nymphs in the wanton adventures. The blood coursed hotly through my veins. I felt the need of something I had never had before; something to cool the burning heat for the first time generated my loins. I put my hand on the seat of desire; the young hair that grew there had not yet become thick enough to protect the lips from the most casual touch. They grew sensitive under my hands. And as I read of the rape or seduction of one of the goddesses after another, my fingers slipped in between my lips and by a gentle movement they afforded me some pleasure.

'This motion, to be satisfactory, had to be constantly increased, and when I came to the raptures of Venus in the arms of Mars, my wantonness became uncontrollable. A sensation such as described in the book partly thrilled me; I plunged my fingers in the full length to complete it, and away went my maiden-head. It hurt me cruelly, but I did not care for that; I know the irreparable injury my folly had caused; I was disgusted with my wantonness, and flung the book away. I never put my fingers on that place again, much less let any man touch me. One night I told my husband all the pitiful truth, but he was still suspicious. We lived in Naples; he was a professor in the university. He seemed to think of nothing but science. For two or three weeks together he would go to bed and rise again without even having put his hand under my chemise, and still more rarely gave me the marital embrace. But I did not suffer myself to care for that. One day I accompanied him on a journey to another town to look for some rare old manuscripts of which he had heard. We were going along a lonely road through a forest when a large and gaily dressed brigand stepped from the woods and stopped us. "Resist at your peril," he said, pointing a cocked pistol at us and leading the horse and vehicle into a lonely side path. When he had got some distance from the main road he stopped and ordered us to get out.

'He fastened the horse to a tree and then took some cord from his pocket, with which he firmly bound my husband's hands behind his back, and having also tied his feet together, he bound him to a tree and searched him for valuables. "Now, my fair lady," he said, approaching me, "it is your turn."

"'Take my jewellery," I begged, "it is all I have, and let us go."

"'Thank you for the present," he replied, "but you have something else I prize still more." Then he put his arm around my waist and attempted to kiss me.

'I struggled to get free, while my husband alternately cursed and entreated him. But all to no purpose. I tried to get close to my husband, but it only served to make him a closer witness to what followed. I was suddenly tripped and thrown to the ground with the brigand on top of me. He held both of my hands on the ground above my head with one of his own; with the other he tore open the front of my dress and exposed my bosoms, which he fondled with his hand and sucked with his mouth.

'Then he pulled up the skirts of my dress and petticoat. I redoubled my exertion, and even got one of my hands loose; by this time he had forced open my thighs with his knee and lay between them. He pinioned both of my hands as before, leaving one of his own free to get his shaft and push it into me.

'Then every struggle I made seemed to work it in further. I could only sob with rage and shame; the brigand with his Herculean strength did his will with me right before my husband's eyes, who by this time had howled himself hoarse with curses.

'Angry and mortified as I was it began to feel good; to escape this crowning humiliation I made one great

effort to get free. I was pinioned to the ground by a fierce thrust of my ravisher, and then I felt the cream of his strength entering my loins. The sensation almost thrilled me; but his powerful grasp became so relaxed that by a great effort I extricated myself from beneath him. I ran to my husband and began untying him, but the brigand seized me by the wrists and dragged me some distance up the pathway. Then he suddenly thrust his hand into my bosom and gave it a hard squeeze; kissed my averted face and let me go. I ran back, trembling and sobbing, to my husband, whom I unbound as rapidly as possible. He unfastened the horse without saying a word or even helping me into the vehicle and drove home in silent and sullen gloom.

'It was too cruel. I had been able to endure his suspicions with regard to the loss of my maiden-head, because it had been the result of my own folly. But this dreadful rape had been committed through no fault of mine. He never afterward lay with me or held me in his embrace, although we continued to live together. A young woman in the bloom of vigour, and just well enough initiated into the mysteries of matrimony, I was condemned to celibacy.

'Wanton thoughts occupied my mind until my sheath would throb and its lips moisten and swell with desire for hours together. I resorted to the means which had despoiled my maiden-head, but it was little more than constant agitation. My husband suspected me and I determined to give him cause. It seemed as if no one man could satisfy me now; I longed for an opportunity to give rein to my passions. At this time the Russian fleet came into the harbour. My sister's husband was a naval attaché at Naples, and it fell to him to entertain the Russian officers. So my sister gave a masked ball to which they were invited. My husband would not go, but he made no objections to my attending and staying all night at my sister's house. My room opened upon the passage that connected the ball room with the conservatory, and I could not get into it without being observed. I procured a long and ample nun's robe, which covered me from my throat to my toes; it also had a hood which covered my head and face.

'Under this disguise I wore the dress, or rather, the undress of a dancing girl; a cloth of gold and a skirt of the thinnest lawn were absolutely the only articles of which it consisted besides my stockings and slippers; the vest had no sleeves or shoulders, and exposed my bosom clear to the nipples; if I moved quickly the short and gauzy skirt showed my naked thighs. As soon as the guests began to mingle on the floor I touched the arm of a stalwart Russian officer; he, like the other guests, was masked, but I knew he was a Russian by his hair.

'"Follow me," I whispered. We entered the passageway described, and finding it clear, led him to my room.

'"What a dainty bower," he said in French. "Will it's sweet-voiced occupant be pleased to unmask?" He removed his own mask and disclosed one of those ruddy countenances with bright blue eyes and fair hair which always so bewitched an Italian lady.

'I flung off my nun's disguise and stood revealed to

him in the costume of a lascivious dancing girl.

'The young Russian seemed to admire my dark Italian complexion and I admired his northern hue.

'He knelt and kissed my hand. "Can you pity a bride," said I, "whose husband neglects her?" The flush of pleasure which crossed the officer's face made my eyes seek the floor. "It would be the supremest happiness," he replied, "to pity and console you."

'As he clasped his arms around me our lips met. The moment I had so long desired had now come.

'I was borne in his arms to the bed, where I lay palpitating with desire, while he stripped off his outer garments. Then the fervour of our kisses and caresses showed the length of time we had both suffered without an embrace. My dress formed no obstacle to his access to my bosom, which he seemed to fairly devour, or to my thighs, which he squeezed and patted. I guided his shaft with one hand, while with the other I parted the hair-encircled lips to receive it. How stiff it was, and yet how full of life and warmth; how tight and yet how soft and lubricated was the place it was entering. I was so eager I had not affected to be coy. "How delicious!" he exclaimed. "How exquisite!" I replied. He gave a thrust which enabled me to take his shaft to the hilt; then he gave another and another, each successive one more greedily swallowed; flesh and blood could no longer endure the rapture that was concentrated at my loins; I thrilled from my womb to my very finger tips; I melted and bathed his hot crest; his responsive gush drenched my glowing womb. It seemed as if we were being fused together at the point of contact; then our muscles relaxed loosely in the moisture and we engaged for a while in voluptuous repose. "Now kiss me and go," said I, "and if you value the favour I have granted, you will leave this house at once." My object was to fill his place with another handsome Russian, who might come fresh to the encounter, and whose genitals my wanton hands might explore and my lascivious desire ravish. Months of longing were to be supplied by one night of boundless lust. Six times more before the ball broke up I took a Russian officer to my room and dismissed him as before, and each time a different one; each moisture mingled with Russian sperm. The next morning my glass showed me I had dark and sunken circles around my eyes, and I was somewhat languid, but for a few days at least I was not troubled with desire.'

The fat and charming Italian lady had been gently fondling my genitals all the time she had been speaking and my shaft had begun to rise at the delicate attention. When she finished her story she knelt before me with her forehead on the carpet, laughingly saying as she did so, 'Salaam alirkoum', which was the Moorish to signify that she was at my service. Her large round buttocks were elevated in the air and looked so temptingly smooth and soft that I mounted her in that position as a stallion would mount a mare. She seemed nothing loath, and my half-stiffened shaft worked its way in between the swollen lips past the extraordinary protuberance which my fingers had discovered and buried itself amid the moist and clinging folds of her sheath. My loins sank into her fat buttocks, which yielded as I pushed, until my glands were hidden in her hair like eggs in a nest. Still I kept with the delightful sensation and my crest exchanged a wanton desire with her womb. I held her firmly by clasping her great soft bosoms in either hand. A few minutes more and I would have paid tribute to her voluptuous loins, but Laura could not wait: with a sigh of satisfaction her frame became limp, her knees gave way and she sank flat on her belly; my shaft drew out of her more stiff than it went in. The same accompanying sucking noise that ended my connection with Helene set them all to laughing. 'I must take a measurement,' said one of them, and taking off her bracelet she clasped it around my shaft, but the clasp would not fasten; the bracelet was not large enough. Then they all tried their bracelets with the same result. 'How shall we get its length?' said one of them. 'Four of you have the measure already,' said I, 'and you know I promised it to all of you. Please let me take some measurements now,' I added, unwinding the garter from the leg of the nearest lady; it was a piece of strong tape and suited my purpose admirably. I measured the height of all their bosoms and the circumference of their thighs, and then, amid laughing protestations, I parted the hair between each of their thighs and measured the length of their slits. In this last measurement they all seemed to be desirous of being the smallest, as in the others they each wished to the largest in size.

A young Persian who was introduced later in the even bore off the palm in the contest. Her diminutive slit looked all the more cunning that the hair around it was hardly long enough to curl.

Zuleika had the largest bosoms, while the thighs of Laura defied competition. 'Here, Anna, take the scarf,' interrupted the Italian, 'and tell the Captain something about Circassia.' The lady thus addressed was about nineteen years old, and she was tall and slender; her limbs were finely tapered, and so was her round waist, which I could have spanned with my two hands; her beautifully cut bosoms were as erect as if they had been carved from alabaster, which her skin resembled in whiteness. The hair on her small head was of the palest blonde, but that of her loins was fiery red, which I had heard was a sign of uncontrollable wantonness; if so, this lady's face gave no indication of it; her large blue eyes looked at me with the innocence of childhood, and the delicate roseate hue of her cheeks varied at every changing emotion. She did not seem insensible, however, to the privilege conferred upon her by the scarf; she laid herself between my thighs, where she leaned with her elbow on the cushion, supporting her graceful head with her hand; her breasts rested on my loins and my shaft was imprisoned by her snowy bosoms, from between which its red crest peeped out, while she looked me in the face and told her lascivious story.

THE CIRCASSIAN LADY'S STORY

'The powerful old chief to whom mother was married had no children of his own. I was her only child by a former marriage, and her fondness was all centred on me; our religion, which was Greek, forbade a plurality of wives. The old chief was not likely to have a direct heir, and as he was then seventy her great object was to have him confer on me the succession to the principality. At last he agreed to do so if she would countenance his amours with other women; she consented to this, and the strange compact was formed. I was present, but unknown to either of them I had been in the habit for a long time of frequenting a little alcove in their bedroom, where a few books were kept. It was separated by a curtain from the rest of the room, and communicated also with my chamber by a sliding panel; this secret panel which I had accidentally discovered was of a kind often met with in such old castles as we inhabited; it was known to me alone; or, if the old chief knew it, he never thought of it. I had there witnessed all the secrets of the marriage chamber, and of course my passions were rapidly developed.

'My mother was still plump and handsome; she enjoyed keenly the marriage embrace, but always had to work very hard in order to finish the tardy rapture of the old chief. On the occasion of the compact I heard her tell him he could not give her all she wanted. He only replied that a man liked variety. "Very well," she said, "make out the deed of Anna's succession and I will not only countenance, but assist, in your amours. We can in that way at least secure secrecy and avoid a scandal, for no one will suspect a wife of conniving to her husband's amours." The old chief then confided to her that the present object of his desire was Leuline, the handsome wife of the steward of the castle. The next morning I was at my post early. My mother had already managed it with Leuline. She was a large and voluptuous woman, with dark hair and blue eyes, her bosoms were not much developed, but her thighs were immense. She got into bed with my mother and pretended to be asleep when the old chief came in. He undressed, got into bed with them and mounted Leuline, who lay with her head on my mother's arm close to her bosom. An expression of pleasure stole over Leuline's face, which became more ineffable at every thrust. At last their mingled sighs and stillness which followed gave proof that the embrace had been mutually satisfactory.

"'You can imagine," said Anna, smiling at the other girls, "how I longed for the embrace of a man just then." Plans for future meetings, and jokes at the expense of Leuline's husband, together with explorations of Leuline's charms, filled up the time till the old chief's staff grew stiff again; he once more plunged it into Leuline's great loins, who enjoyed it so highly that she finished and left him in the lurch. I could hardly restrain myself, I so longed for the thrusts that were wasted on Leuline. My mother must have felt the same way for she asked the old chief to let her finish him. He had more than once sucked on her fine bosoms during the onset; he now transferred his crimson crest, dripping with Leuline's moisture. The energy with which my mother received him made me fairly wriggle my loins in sympathy. She wound her arms around him and played up her loins to meet his descending thrusts; then their frames were convulsed for a few moments with the culminary rapture and they subsided into perfect repose.

'I had often before felt wanton emotions at my post of observation; I wanted a man, and that immediately. I was about to seek one of the sentinels at his post and confer my virginity on the first rude soldier I met in the cover of the ramparts when I remembered Teasidor, a young priest who was attached to the chapel of the castle. He was a delicate looking boy of about seventeen, with a countenance that indicated the purity of his character. I went to his room and softly knocked on the door. To my timid knock the answer was delayed; when at last he said, "Come in," I saw that he had employed the interval in slipping on a night gown, for he had been just about to retire. He looked astonished; as well he might, when he saw me. "I have come to make a confession and ask your counsel," I said. "Had we not better go to the chapel?" he asked.

"'It is better here," I replied, "for the subject is a worldly one, though of much importance to me. I love a young man who is indifferent to my preference; nay, he is insensible that it is he that I love. I would have my parents hint to him that his address would be accepted, but I shall have to marry a soldier and he is not one. What shall I do?"

"'Strive to forget him, my lady," was the answer.

'I stood for a moment with my eyes cast on the floor and my cheeks burning, and then I cried: "Cruel man, it is you who has my heart!" My head dropped forward. I seemed about to fall, but I put up my mouth for the kiss which he bent to impress upon it. Regrets were then mingled with kisses, as I allowed my wrapper to partly open and expose my bosoms; he ventured timidly to kiss them; his kisses became more and more ardent; I had got him at last where a man has no conscience. He stretched himself on the bed beside me, he took me in his arms, our lips were glued together. As much by my contriving as his own, though he did not do it, my wrapper and dressing gown opened and a skirt and chemise were all that separated a stiff object from my thighs. Fired by lust as I was, I had shame enough left to leave the removal of these slight things to him. I could hardly wait upon his timidity. I must have been the first woman he had ever entered, for he was very awkward in guiding his crest to the lips that yearned to close upon it.

'It was a small thing, but very stiff. At last it penetrated me a little way and I felt the touch of his crest against my maiden-head like an electric shock; it set all my nerves to tingling with pleasure. I could no longer even feign modesty. I involuntarily wrapped my arms around him, and he gave the fatal thrust; his little crest pierced through my maiden-head with a cutting pain which I felt no more than a bulling heifer would have felt the stroke of a switch; the pain was drowned in overwhelming pleasure, the thrill swept over every fibre of my frame; not only at the first thrust, but three times successively, and at each plunge I gave a sigh of rapture; then my tense muscles relaxed and I received with pleasure at least a dozen more strokes. Something more was wanting; it was the gush of sperm that Teasidore at last poured into my heated sheath like balm. He sank heavily upon me for a few minutes with his face buried in my neck. I was enjoying a voluptuous languor, then I felt his little shrunken staff floating out of my sheath with mingled blood and sperm. Remorse had already seized him; he raised himself on his elbow and gazed pitifully into my face. I was blushing, so I covered my face with my hands. "I have ruined you!" he said, "wretch that I am! Heaven will never forgive me!" He got up from the bed without even giving me another kiss and knelt before his crucifix. "Will you not join me in asking heaven for mercy on my sin?" he said.

'I made some excuse and fled from the room. The next morning I heard that he had gone to join a convent far up in the mountain. By this time I had come to the conclusion that I had let him off too quickly; I had not had enough. Perhaps a warm bath would help to soothe me. We had a large bath half the size of a room, and deep enough when full to cover my breasts. It had a door into my room, and also into my mother's who at this time in the morning was busy with her servants. It was the old chief's time to take a bath, and as he always had the water, I determined to share it with him. I had heretofore doubted whether the old chief would want to touch his wife's daughter, but my success with the young priest gave me courage. I took all my clothes in my room and peeped through the door; he was floating on his back playing with his shaft; it dangled limber in the water. I had almost always seen it stiff, and I promised myself the pleasure of getting it in condition, which I preferred. Pretty soon he came to the side toward me where he could not be seen by me. Now was the time for me to come in as if I did not know he was there. I opened my door suddenly and ran and jumped into the water.

'I swam across the bath, turned around and became the picture of astonishment at seeing him. I first covered my face with my hands; then my bosom with one hand and my loins with the other. I didn't scream; that might bring my mother. Then I turned my back on him. The side of the bath where I stood was perpendicular; he stood by the sloping side where we got out; of course I had to stay. "It's all right, Anna," he said, "we will have a nice bath together." I tried to dodge past him but he caught me.

"I shall scream," I said; but of course I didn't.

'I was fast in his arms, his stiffening staff crushing against my buttocks and one of his hands squeezing each of my bosoms. My apprehensions of reluctance on his part had all departed, so I kept up more show of resistance; I struggled to get away, but at length he turned my face toward him; this brought my back to the sloping side of the bath tub, against which he pressed me. Half standing and half lying, my head was still above the water; the wantonness of the situation and the warmth of the water made the bath seem like a voluptuous sea. Of course I had put both my arms around him to keep from sinking; his hands were thus both at liberty; he needed them both to work his stiffened shaft into me.

'Leuline and my mother only the night before had taken the starch out of it; nothing but the excitement of such a kind of rape would have stiffened it at all; half limber as it was, it completely filled me, paining me a little at first, but gradually feeling better and better, pervaded all through with the most lascivious sensation, the warm water churning in and out of my sheath at every thrust, ministering to my lust. All the bath water seemed to be of the male gender, and all of it embracing me and adding to my ecstasy. For fully five minutes I abandoned myself to the delicious dissolving feeling not of thrilling as the young priest had caused the night before, but more prolonged, even after it had subsided and died away, the plunges of the old chief were pleasant. Finally his shaft became for a moment rigid deep within me, he gave a throb or two which deprived him of his strength and he no longer supported me. I scrambled from his arms up the side of the bath, regained my own room, shut the door and sank exhausted on the bed. We never pursued the intrigue, as the terror of my mother was too much before our eyes; besides, a few days later I was engaged in an amour with Duloff, the handsome young captain of the guards, while the old chief had another bedfellow besides my mother.

'This time I saw it was a young maid who timidly blushed in the place of the blooming Leuline, for still soft and lubricated was the place it was entering. It was some time afterward the old chief was slain in battle, and the sagacity of my mother was rewarded.

'I succeeded peacefully to the principality, but my mother swayed the real power; I was willing she should do so provided she did not interfere with my amours, it was on her advice that I didn't marry,

'"A virgin chieftain will be popular with the people, and you can control far better unmarried," she told me. And it was so. Ruloff, the captain of the guards, was my abject slave; so also was Cassim and Selim, two of the bravest young chiefs in the army. I admitted them all to my bed in turn. Ruloff the most frequent, for he was powerfully built and naturally had genitals correspondingly large. When I desired to be tickled deeply, the tall and slender Selim received the secret summons. It was agreeable sometimes to be stretched without being deeply penetrated. Each of them suspected the other two also enjoyed my favours, but they were not certain. One evening I invited them all to my secret apartments; the sideboard had been replenished, the servants dismissed for the night and the doors locked. I was dressed in a purple velvet bodice and a petticoat of red silk.

'I had on my richest lace and jewellery, and the crown of the principality was on my brow. The three officers glittered in their splendid uniforms; suspense and curiosity were mingled in their countenance. I waited until several toasts had been drunk in my honour and my wantonness devoured the fine young men and thus addressed them: "Should not a Circassion princess have as many privileges as a Turkish Pasha?"

"'Certainly," they all replied. "Should she not be entitled to a harem as well as he?"

"'Yes," they answered, hesitating.

"'Then you shall be lord of the lips." The polite young officer set the example of devotion by coming to my side and kissing the lips that I had committed to his care. "You, Selim, are lord of the bosom." He came upon the other side of me and kissed the bosom which peeped out above the lace of my bodice. "You, Ruloff, shall be lord of the thighs." He was not to be outdone in loyalty; he knelt before me, and raising my skirt, planted a kiss on the hairy mouth it concealed; then I felt his tongue penetrate the lips beneath it, causing a flush of desire to surge through my frame.

"'Let us divest ourselves of this clothing which makes mortals of us, and become like the ancient gods," I said. My example, together with the champagne, now broke down all reserve. We stripped entirely naked and amused ourselves by imitating the attitudes usually given by art to the most celebrated heathen divinities. It was not enough for me to compare the forms of the young men by observation; I freely caressed and handled their genitals till they lost all restraint and gathered so closely about me that I was squeezed in their joint embrace. I flung my arms around Cassim and bade him lie down on his back with me on top of him; his loins were elevated higher than his head by a pile of cushions on which he lay. I

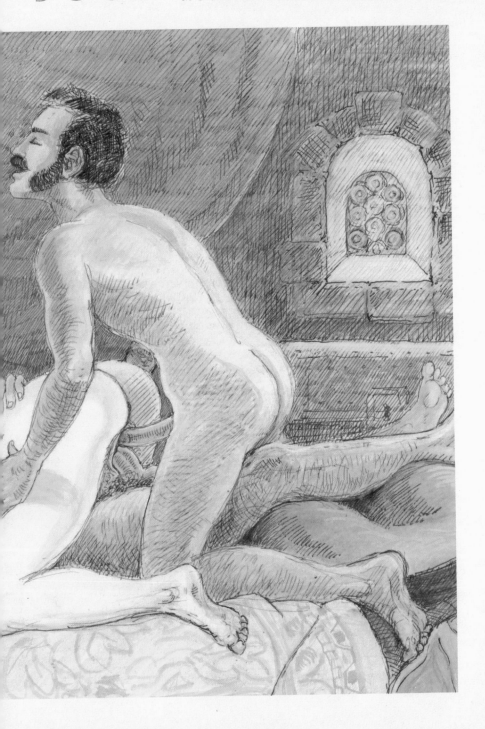

worked backward while he guided his shaft completely into me; my buttocks presenting a fair mark to Selim, who mounted me behind and slowly worked his shaft into the same orifice that Cassim had already entered. It was the tightest kind of fit.

'The first entrance had stirred my desire to a flame and made me welcome the second with greediness. Cassim's position was such that he could hardly stir, but Selim plunged his long and slender shaft into me again and again with thrusts that required all his strength; my sheath was stretched to its utmost tension by the two shafts, but all its distended nerves quivered with lust. Ruloff now knelt close in front of me with his knee on either side of my head. I lay a moment with my flushed cheeks on his genitals; then I grasped his shaft in my hand and played rapidly up and down on it; Cassim, with his arm wrapped around my waist, was sucking my bosom. Selim squeezed my thighs in his grasp at every thrust he gave. I felt my crisis coming; overwhelming three-fold intensity inspired by the contact of three such vigorous men at once; in my wild abandon I sucked Ruloff's crest in my mouth. Then I thrilled and melted with a groan that resounded through the room; all three of the young men followed me to the realms of bliss of which I soared, my sheath overflowed with the double tribute which jetted and spurted and gushed in it; my mouth was filled with Ruloff's sperm; both pairs of my lips were dripping, my whole frame seemed saturated with the exquisite moisture.

'As the mingled sighs of the young men, which echoed

to my prolonged groans of rapture, died away, I sank into a semi-conscious state, from which I did not rise that evening; it was a deep, dreamy, voluptuous repose which an occasional smarting sensation in my sheath did not disturb. The wine and profuse organs had done their work. The young men put me to bed and quietly dispersed. It was the only time I had my harem; the next day our troops lost a battle, the great castle was taken by the enemy and I was on my way to the slave market.'

Anna thus finished her story, my shaft peeped out from between her bosoms, and it was now stiff with desire. The fat Italian had aroused its vitality, though she had failed to extract any tribute from it.

My glands had again filled while I listened to the innocent Circassian's passionate tale. Still holding her between my thighs, I turned so as to bring her back beneath me. Then, changing and adjusting my thighs between hers, I parted the fiery red hair that concealed lips equally fiery and commenced the onset. The delicious heat and moisture set the blood to dancing in my veins; my crest lingered a moment at the lips, and then glided into the clinging folds of her sheath. When I had completely entered it gave a convulsive contraction round my shaft and Anna melted. Indeed, the ladies were all ripe to the melting point, and I had to rally repeatedly to meet their fresh, successive ardour. Anna became passive, but she still seemed to enjoy the deep rapid thrusts; for several moments I continued to thrust into her white loins; at every thrust I became more furious.

I buried my hilt again and again, in the vain effort to touch her womb; I felt that if my crest could only reach that far up her long and slender body, I would consummate the exquisite connection. She seemed to divine my wish; she opened her thighs and, drawing her knees upward, wrapped her long slender legs around my waist with a strength of which I had not thought her capable.Fixing my eyes on her sweet face, I gave another plunge. She was so fairly exposed to my thrusts that I rammed her womb clear up in her belly. The sperm gushed from my crest in consecutive jets and I gave a sigh of perfect satisfaction. I was completely exhausted. My nervous frame stretched itself at full length upon her and I sank into a voluptuous languor that gradually turned into sleep. I slept for fully an hour, the ladies told me when I awoke, and I felt the vigour returning. They brought me some sherbert and confections which refreshed me, and one of them was so considerate as to point out to me where to make water. Then I heard that Anna had thrown the scarf so that it fell on the shoulders of two young girls and would not tell them which was to keep it, but mischievously referred it to me. Leaving the disorder to the chapter of incidents, I begged them both to favour us with a story. It was a Portuguese girl named Virginia who began. She was a pretty little creature not more than fourteen years old, and very small for her age. Her slight limbs were beautifully rounded, and tapered to the most cunning little feet and hands; her pretty bosoms, though small, were perfect hemispheres; her hair was very dark and braided into strands which were carefully coiled up under a slender comb; her complexion was dark, but her large, fiery eyes indicated some northern blood.

THE PORTUGUESE LADY'S STORY

'My father was an English wine merchant at Lisbon and my mother was a Portuguese lady; I was the only child, but there was a little boy named Diego, two years older than I, who came to live with us when I was ten. I subsequently found that he was the fruit of my father's amours before his marriage; but, as Diego's mother was dead, my mother naturally let him have a home with us. Diego and I were the best of friends. Among other amusements, a favourite play with us was getting married.

'Diego knew quite enough to play this when no one was by, and he always finished by getting on me! His little organ would hardly get stiff enough to penetrate me, but he must have gradually obliterated all traces of a maiden-head, for I cannot remember ever having one. There was no consummation in our connection; neither of us were ripe enough for that, but there were charms about it which made us keep it up at intervals for a year or two. One evening Diego proposed, and I agreed, that we should postpone being together after our little ceremony of marriage until we went to bed. This occurred the day after I had noticed the appearance of some marks of my monthly period on my shirt. Our rooms were adjoining, and after I had got nearly asleep that night, for I had forgotten all about it, Diego came in; he crept into bed, and getting on top of me inserted his little organ as usual; being both undressed it felt better than ever before, and we explored each other's naked forms with our hands; my bosoms for the first time attracted Diego's attention; they were quite little, but it gave me as much pleasure to have them fondled and kissed as it seemed to give him to do it, for Portuguese blood matures young.

'I began to have a feeling in my sheath. Diego's little shaft being in it so still did not satisfy; I gave a push upwards with my loins, he returned it with a thrust which felt pleasant; he kept thrusting incessantly for many minutes, and all the time it became more delightful, yet I longed for the thrusts to become more deep and rapid. "Isn't it splendid?" I whispered. "Do it harder."

'"It's perfectly splendid," he answered, in a voice almost inarticulate with rapture. For two or three minutes we kept up the rapid motion, when I felt Diego's little shaft growing stiffer than ever before; the delight he afforded me was so exquisite that I culminated in a long, sweet and refreshing thrill; Diego must have melted at the same time and paid the first tribute of his scanty drops; we both of us fairly whined with excitement and delight at our unexpected success. The noise brought my mother to the room; she caught us lying exhausted in each other's arms, she took off her slipper and scourged Diego back to his room, then she turned down the bed clothes and spanked my bottom thoroughly, and having locked the door of my room and his, left me to my reflections. The next morning Diego was sent to Brazil. My parents at once began to look around for a suitable match for me, fearing doubtless, that I might seek another opportunity to gratify my precocious passions. They fixed upon a nobleman who was attracted by my father's wealth, and they promised him my hand. He was dissipated, but so were all the young men of Lisbon. He was quite good-looking, and though I had seen him but a few times, I looked forward to the marriage with pleasure, for I longed for another such delightful experience as I had had with Diego. At length the bridal evening came; the ceremony was performed in the presence of many guests and was followed by dancing and the popping of champagne corks until a late hour, when the bridesmaids put me to bed. I did not have to wait long for my husband; he came in somewhat under the influence of wine, hurriedly took off his clothes and hardly waited to kiss and embrace me before he exercised his marital rights.

'I was penetrated by a little object not as big as Diego's! Before I had recovered from my surprise and disappointment he had accomplished his purpose and sank down beside me to sleep. I shed bitter tears of chagrin. Several times every night for two or three weeks, the same strange connections took place, differing only that he was not immediately overcome with sleep. Only once during that time did my constantly aroused and disappointed passion succeed in culminating quick enough to melt, and that only partially. I dared not question him, for that would betray the experience I had. One night I purposefully left the lamp burning and waited for him to get into a sound sleep; then I turned the bed clothes down and examined his organ; it was a mere scarred remnant which had evidently been eaten away by disease; it was only capable of erection by great effort; no wonder he was constantly subject to the torture of his disappointed desires. After this I shunned him as much as possible, finding no solace in company with him and constantly subjected to the torture of his disappointed desires. Oh, for an entire man! I sighed. He took himself nearly every night to the gambling table.

'Early one evening he went off as usual; I retired to my bedroom and looked out through the window blind; our house, like many others in Lisbon, was built in the form of a quadrangle, the rear of which was the stable. If I sat on one side of my window I could see one side of the stable wall, and I could only be seen from it. There was only one window in it, which served for Pedro, the coachman, who was admitted to many privileges, for there is no prejudice against colour in Portugal.

'Pedro was the most gigantic coachman in the city; indeed, he was the largest well-proportioned man I had ever seen in my life. As I looked out through the blind I distinctly saw him gazing at my window. I at once determined to have sport; standing before the glass beside the window, I lighted the lamp as if unconscious of observation; indeed, I could not have been seen from any other quarter than Pedro's window, and that was smaller and higher than mine; I threw open the blind as for air, and began slowly to undress; then I stood in my chemise and petticoat, lazily brushing my hair before the glass, which displayed my naked arms and bosoms to good advantage. Then I sat down to take off my shoes, and lifted my foot to my knee for convenience in untying them. My hidden observer must have seen under my petticoat up to my loins and perhaps an inch inside of them, for my legs were stretched very wide apart. I grew wanton with the thought of the influence I had made by this time on his passions; if his desires were not thoroughly aroused it was no fault of mine. I stood before the glass again and let my petticoat and chemise fall to the floor, but delayed putting on my night-gown. I yawned and fondled my breasts with my hands as a woman does, giving, as I did so, an undulating motion to my loins.

'Soon I heard a soft and heavy tread coming from the coach room stairs towards my door. I might have locked it, but I did not. Was this not just what I had been praying for? The door opened and Pedro entered; I held up my night-gown before my naked form. "If I am too bold, my lady," he said, in great agitation, "bid me go and I will cast myself into the river." He need not have been half so tragic.

'"Pedro," said I, "have you no more politeness than to keep on your clothes when a lady is undressed?" His anxious countenance relaxed at once into a reassured smile, and he gallantly kissed my hand; my lips he did not presume to kiss at all. Then he undressed himself without stopping till his Herculean form stood entirely naked before me in all its gigantic and magnificent proportions; his immense shaft was proudly erect and huge even for a giant; pendant from it hung glands which seemed to my somewhat startled eyes as large as a coconut. He lifted me without an effort till my bosoms were opposite his mouth, into which he almost entirely sucked one of them; my legs wound themselves around his waist and I found myself sitting on the crest of his great stiff shaft, which was directly under the lips of my sheath, and it slowly entered them. At last I was penetrated by an organ which I could hardly accommodate; then I looked in the mirror, before which we were standing. At least half of his great shaft was plainly visible below my buttocks; he appeared like a great statue of ebony, bearing at his bosom one of ivory. I worked my loins, but I could plainly see by the mirror Pedro was heading rapidly to a blissful termination; at this he laid me on my back on the bed without losing our connection, and bracing his feet against the footboard, gave an irresistible plunge; it seemed to ram my womb clear up under my bosom; my whole body seemed only a sheath quivering with lascivious gratification; I bore with out flinching two more such plunges and then came the overwhelming thrill; in the midst of it I felt the gushing sperm spurting like fountain in my belly; we subsided simultaneously with a long drawn breath, Pedro at once considerately relieving me of his great weight. Twice before he left I was spurred on by desire to court the brunt of his tremendous onset,

and then I made him go. I was completely gorged and sated. Three days afterwards we had to fly together to escape imminent discovery threatened by my maid. We safely reached the African coast.'

When the pretty little Portuguese finished her story I exchanged kisses with her; so did I with her companion on the other side of me.

My crest was rising, but another story would give it time to be fully ready. 'My friend's name is Myrzella, and she is a Persian,' said Virginia, receiving another kiss for her information. Myrzella, of course was kissed when she was named. She was still younger than Virginia. The pink slit between her thighs was set off by the faintest trace of hair; it looked like a delicate seashell. She was quite plump, her thighs were nearly the size of Virginia's, her bosoms were developed as much as those of a northern girl several years later in life, her hair was black and glossy as a raven's wing, descending in two braids to the calves of her legs when she stood erect; her eyes were black as her hair, large and sparkling, but full of tenderness; her cheeks had little colour except under emotion, but her lips were crimson red.

THE PERSIAN LADY'S STORY

'My home until two months ago was on the Tigris. I was captured by Turks when on a journey to meet my affianced husband, whom I had never seen.

'Our party was on horseback proceeding along the bank of the river when the Turkish bandits pounced upon us. There was a flash of sabers and a volley of pistol shots which dispersed my friends, and my horse was seized by the bridle and hurried to the water's edge; there was a boat waiting which conveyed us to the Turkish shore. I soon found myself an inmate of the harem of the fierce bandit who had captured me, there were four other women in the harem, among whom I was allowed to rest and refresh myself with supper, though I could eat but little. Then the Turk came into the apartment. He was a man of middle age, upon whose countenance was written the most brutal passions. I fairly loathed the sight of him and hoped I would soon be ransomed. He put his arms around me and attempted to kiss me, but I shrank from his embrace. "She would prefer to have you undress her," he said to the women, who seemed to enjoy the spectacle of my unwilling espousal. They soon took everything off but my chemise, while the Turk stripped himself perfectly naked, and for the first time, and under interesting circumstances, I saw the genitals of a man. They were excited by lust to a size I could never have imagined. He again tried to take me in his arms, but I struggled so that my chemise was torn off and I cowered naked on the floor; he bade the women hold me; each of my feet and each of my hands were held by one of the four and I lay on my back with my arms and legs stretched apart. As I lay there panting with my struggles, he got upon me and entered me with one fierce and brutal thrust which tore away my maidenhead with a pang of excruciating agony. With a tremendous effort I got one of my hands loose from the woman who held it and seized the Turk's dagger, which lay clear upon the pile of clothing he had taken off: the women all let me go and the Turk jumped off before he had time to repeat his thrust. I sprang to a corner of the room in an agony of shame and rage, ready to kill the first who touched me. The Turk stood grasping his stiff shaft, all stained with blood; his baffled lust sought the first object on which to vent itself.

"'Lie down, Achmet," he said, "I must have a tight place to finish what I have begun of her." The person addressed lay belly downward, and then the Turk turned up the female petticoat which had heretofore concealed the male sex of the wearer; it was indeed a boy, doubtless a eunuch whom the Turk kept to supplement the service of the three women of his harem. On the prostate form of this boy the Turk mounted, and the grunts of satisfaction soon proclaimed that he had satisfied his brutal lust. I thanked heaven that I had not

suffered him to finish in me. After a while he arose and pulled the petticoat over the boy's buttocks, who again appeared in the semblance of a women. "Lock up that little tiger cat in a room by herself," said the Turk, pointing to me. I was glad to be alone, and went into the room indicated without any opposition.

'I looked around for something to put on; the only articles I could see was a rich suit of boy's clothing which doubtless belonged to the one in the next room. I dressed myself in these, completing my disguise by concealing my hair under the boy's turban. Then I looked from the window to see what were the chances of escape; though the room was on the second floor it was not very high from the ground, which I reached very easily. Then I made my way to the river and got into a boat that was moored at the bank; casting it loose I floated down the stream; the night was dark and my boat was nearly run down by a passing vessel, I loudly called for aid and was taken on board where I breathed freely again. The vessel sailed down the Persian river, and crossed over to the Red Sea, at last reaching the shore of Egypt. I found my way to Alexandria in company with some merchants, one of whom took fancy to me and engaged me as an attendant. He owned the ship on which we sailed from the former port. We were the only occupants of the cabin. He was a handsome young man and he won my heart by his uniform kindness, but I did not reveal the secret of my sex. The day before we reached Morocco he called me into his cabin to assist him in his bath. He stripped unconcernedly before me; his form was manly and graceful, but I was fascinated with the organs which were peculiar to his sex; they hung drooping at his loins, unconscious that a woman was looking at them, nay, touching them, for I contrived to touch as often as I could while I bathed him. When I had finished sponging him he lay extended on the sofa for me to rub him dry. My hands explored all parts of his person, but lingered longest at his thighs, so much so that his shaft began to rise at the friction. "Take care, little fellow," said he, "you will arouse a passion you cannot gratify." I felt my cheeks burning; a soft desire ran through my veins, and I was about to open my bosom and reveal my sex, but the thoughts of the terrible pang in the Turkish harem restrained me. I stooped and kissed his thighs, my cheeks brushing against his genitals; then I sat down while he dressed and watched him until the object which so attracted me was concealed by his clothes. The next day we were in port and Pasha Abdallah came on board when his business was finished, and conversation turned on me. "I will make you a present of him," said the young merchant; "poor fellow, it is too bad to keep him at sea." He did not know how dejected I was at this change of masters; but it was no time for explanation. Abdallah took me with him and confided me to his chief eunuch, to whom I sought the first opportunity to reveal my sex and misfortune. I have been with these amiable people a week, but the Pasha has not touched me yet. I suppose that I owe my exemption to the fact that I am not a virgin.'

'But you are to all intents and purposes a virgin, my charming Myrzella,' said I, tightening my arm around her waist and kissing her as she finished speaking. She eluded my grasp and seized Virginia by the hands.

'Come,' she exclaimed, gaily, 'let's have a waltz.' The two pretty little creatures floated around the room in each other's arms, while Inez took up a flute and played a suitable accompaniment. At every complete revolution in the dance, Virginia held Myrzella in a close grasp and their loins were pressed tightly together; their wanton motion was kept up till their already excited passions were completely aroused. They suddenly finished the dance and lay down on the cushions in each other's embrace, with their thighs locked so that the lips between them pressed together; the lips at their loins not only kissed, but their mouths were glued. In this barren embrace I was on top of them both in a twinkling, guiding my shaft between them.

My nap after Anna's exhaustive embrace had restored my vigour; the stories of the young girls had roused my passions; the thought of conferring on Myrzella her first rapture made me feel like a war horse going to battle. My shaft glided between them, entering neither, but it was deliciously moistened by the dewy lips at the loins of both; as I gave another thrust Virginia slyly put one of her hands behind me and guided it into her own sheath; she was on top of Myrzella who was pinioned between the two of us.. My loins were no sooner crushed against Virginia's buttocks than I felt my crest bathed with her melting shower; to me the sensation was exquisite; to her it was final; she sank with a long sigh, perfectly limp, on Myrzella. I drew out my shaft and plunged it, all dripping with Virginia's moisture, into the pretty Persian girl; moist as it was, it entered to the hilt. Virginia's thin buttocks were but little in the way, my hands could fondle both their bosoms at once; my crest, vivified with the moisture of them both, was battering at Myrzella's womb, my kisses were showered on the neck of one and then on the other. My over-wrought nerves could endure no longer, and the gushing sperm came blissfully to a termination; while it was gushing the pretty Persian girl melted with a thrill at her first rapture; her screams of delight were so loud and prolonged that the ladies had to hush her for fear it would alert the guard at the gates. I had just strength enough to turn Virginia over on her back, close beside Myrzella, then clasping them both in my arms, I stretched a leg between the thighs of each, and we lay in voluptuous repose, my forehead resting on the cushions and each girl appropriating one of my cheeks for kisses. 'Do tell us how your maiden-head was taken, Captain,' said one of the ladies, after I had recovered from the exhaustion of my double embrace. 'Sure enough! Why not?' they all cried in chorus. So, setting myself into a luxurious position, more convenient for story telling, and still clasped in the arms of Virginia and Myrzella, I began.

THE CAPTAIN'S FIRST STORY

'When I was a boy there was a beautiful girl named Rosemond, whose family estate in Yorkshire adjoined our own. Though she was seven years older than I, a close but innocent feeling sprang up between us. I was her companion on horseback rides, nutting excursions and country excursions. This intimacy was kept up till suitors began to appear for her hand, to one of whom she was finally married and went to live in London. Soon after I was thirteen I was sent away to school. Rosemond, who had now been married some time, kept a standing invitation for me to visit her. Accordingly I stopped at her house one night on my way through London. Her husband was away and we had full leisure to talk over old times. She had now grown into an elegant woman with a form well developed, and was a fine type of blonde, rosy-cheeked, blue-eyed English matron; my boyish admiration grew more confirmed than ever. After dinner was over, and we were sitting on the sofa together, we grew so confidential that she at last unfolded her troubles to me.

'Her husband, she told me, was unfaithful; he had even then left the city that he might be with another woman; it was probably the first occasion on which she had confided her troubles to anyone; I could hardly understand what she meant; I was as green and innocent as it was possible for a country boy to be, but when I saw her tears I knew she was unhappy, and I drew her head to my shoulder and kissed her. "Do let me console you," I said. My meaning was innocent, but she took it otherwise; I knew, for the crimson mantled over her neck and cheeks. She seemed to come to some sudden determination, for she returned my kisses again and again. It was bedtime and the servants had retired. Rosemond began slowly to loosen her dress at the neck as if making what preparations she might down stairs before retiring. I got a glimpse of two white, plump bosoms; little more was said; we both sat deeply thinking, but my thoughts were still innocent.

'Then she drew up her skirt as ladies sometimes do before retiring and warmed her ankles at the fire; I got a glimpse of two plump calves that were twice as big as when we used to romp through the woods in the country, but I sat profoundly still. "George," she said, rising at last, "I feel lonely tonight, and you may sleep with me if you like."

'"If you will not tell on me," I replied, thinking I was too large a boy to sleep with a woman any more.

'"You can trust me for that," she answered, and led the way up stairs. I told her I thought I would undress in my own room, which I did, and then sheepishly came and got into bed with her. She received me in a close embrace; my frame was clasped in her soft, white arms; only two thicknesses of linen separated it from her glowing form; our lips met in a long, delicious kiss: then for the first time desire shot through my marrow and I felt my shaft stiffen against her belly. I knew now what she wanted. What a triumph it would be to gratify her and mingle my thin blood with the rich blood of this beautiful woman in my embrace. Such was my ignorant idea of the sexual connections but to mingle with her, to pour my whole being into her was what nature imperiously demanded of me. I no longer hesitated to lift up her chemise and get on top of her, my naked little loins sank between her naked thighs, my face was buried in her bosom.

'How it got in I don't know, but my little shaft was taken into the hilt with a sensation more sweet than it had ever entered my imagination to conceive. I tried to get it in deeper; there was plenty of depth unsounded but though she helped me with her clasping arms, it would reach no further; I pushed and pushed with all of my might to do something, I knew not what, when Rosemond gave a deep sigh and lay perfectly still.

"'Have I hurt you, Rosemond?" I anxiously asked. She burst into a merry laugh.

"'Get off for a while," she said, "And let us rest." I did not want to get off at all, but I did so and laid by her side, with my loins and rigid little shaft squeezed up against her plump thigh. It was an hour before she would let me get on again. I spent the time in passionately kissing her cheeks, lips and bosoms, and exploring all the secrets of her person, with my hands. She gave the signal by partly lifting me, and again I sank into her voluptuous form. My shaft was engulfed at the first thrust; I rapidly plunged it in again and again, now guiding it against one side and then against the other of her gaping sheath. The heat and the moisture were more delicious than before,

'I felt something leaving my loins; it jetted from my crest and was lost in the profuse moisture that gushed from Rosemond. My wishes were all realised; I was ravished bodily into her; I gave a groan of ecstasy which explained to me the deep sigh she again heaved, and then I knew no more. When I became conscious again she was standing over me sprinkling water in my face. "How you have frightened me," she said, "you lay so still and looked so pale."

'"I only wanted to lie quiet in you arms," I answered. She folded me tenderly in her arms and I went to sleep with my head pillowed on her bosom and one hand between her thighs. We were virtuous the next morning; she had plucked the fruit before it was ripe and none had grown in the night to replace it; my little shaft would not stiffen at the bidding of her warmest kisses. After breakfast the coach drove up for me and I went off to school.'

'I think it was a shame,' said Inez, 'for a married woman to seduce an innocent boy. How nice it must have been,' remarked Anna, 'to take a sweet little fellow's maiden-head.'

'Do tell up another story, captain,' urged Helene. 'Do,' echoed all the others.

THE CAPTAIN'S SECOND STORY

'When I arrived at the age of fifteen I was a slender stripling, but having had an intrigue with a lady's maid, I fancied myself quite a man of the world.

'One evening I attended the theatre with several other young noblemen. The play was Anthony and Cleopatra. The character of Cleopatra was splendidly sustained by an actress of Irish birth whom I will call Charlotta; she was of colossal size but of perfect proportions; the dark complexion of her lovely face made a good representative of the Egyptian queen, whose voluptuous person and amorous nature she delineated so finely that every man in the house was carried away; yet this magnificent woman was nearly fifty years old; her powerful organisation had triumphed over time. After the play was over we went into the green room and I was introduced to her; the charm of her persona and form lost nothing on a nearer approach, though I detected one or two silver threads among her glossy hair; her eyes had the brilliant sparkle of youth, her lips were plump and red and her teeth were as white as pearls. As soon as she heard my name she manifested deep interest, tender light came in her eyes and the colour heightened in her cheeks as she began to talk of my father. Now, I had heard of the trouble my father gave his friends in his youth by his infatuation with an actress. I could no longer doubt that she stood before me. Charlotta's name was free from scandal, remarkably so for an actress; perhaps her liaison with my father had been her only folly. "Do give a little supper party to meet in my room after the play," she said to me. I promised to do so, and accordingly met there a few actors and patrons of the theatre.

'We had a modest supper, where wit and not wine reigned. I sat next to Charlotta, who seemed hardly able to take her eyes off of me. When the guests began to go I lingered at the door and they went without noticing that I remained. The impulse was mutual to clasp each other in our arms. 'Oh, how I wish that you had been my son; it should have been so!' she exclaimed. I was in no mood to be made a baby of. The grand voluptuous form of the queenly actress aroused far other emotions when it was folded to mine.

'"Is this your room?" I asked, drawing her towards the door. "For shame, George," she said, as crimson blushes spread from her cheeks to her splendid bosoms. She was in the costume of Cleopatra, over which she had thrown a long mantle after the play; this mantle had fallen off. It was evident she had intended no assignation, for she moved reluctantly to the door, but she returned the passionate kiss I planted full on her mouth. So commanding was her height that she had to stoop slightly to do it. As soon as we entered the bedroom she sat down on the bed and covered her face with her hands; I took the opportunity to divest myself of most of my clothes; then I stole up to her and kissed her naked and massive shoulders. She rose to her feet, and taking me in her arms as if I were a baby, she walked back and forth across the room with me.

"'Oh, Georgie, Georgie," she cried, "this is almost incest, but I can deny you nothing; I who have allowed no man to embrace me since those delicious days of long ago!" She still carried me in her arms, walking to and fro. My face was in contact with her great bosoms, each of which was as large as my head. As I passionately kissed them my right had dropped to her thighs, from which it parted the loose oriental drapery and found itself in a shaggy mass of curls. Searching at the bottom of these my fingers found a pair of moist, warm lips; I lifted my face from her bosom and we exchanged a kiss; it differed from those she had heretofore given me; it was as voluptuous as my own, and was prolonged until I felt her lips, which my hand was feeling, begin to swell and grow hot. Charlotta carried me rapidly to the bed; her mood was changed from maternal tenderness to fiery passion; she lay me on my back and sprang upon me; she folded me in her great, muscular arms and her substantial thighs settled on my own; immense as they were, they felt as light as a young girl's. It was her hand which guided my rigid shaft amid the thick profusion of hair till it had fairly entered and was rammed to the hilt by the vibration of her magnificent loins; so firmly was I pinioned to the bed by her great weight that I could not move; I felt as if I were about to be ravished like a woman: it was a new sensation, and as charming as it

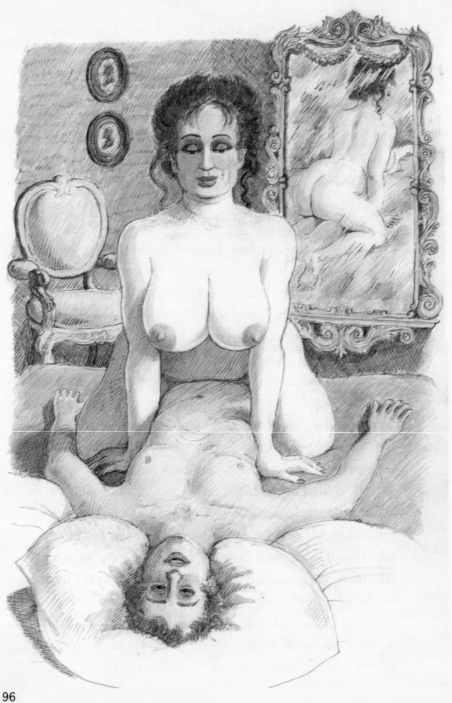

was novel. Charlotta suddenly turned over on her back without relaxing her hold upon me in the least; I found myself on top of her, but she was still mistress of the situation, her arms and legs were wrapped so tightly around me that my bones fairly cracked. It was the rapid undulation of her loins alone that moved our closely joined forms, her mouth was fastened on mine as if she were about to devour me, her big womb pressed against my crest. I felt the crisis coming overwhelmingly in the powerful embrace in which I was held; at this moment her muscles began to relax; with her profuse melting I spent, not with a stinted jet, but with copious gushes which made a suitable tribute to the magnetism of her massive beauty. The rapture lasted in me for some time, even after I became nerveless, and at length died imperceptibly away.

"'Now you must go, you naughty boy," said Charlotta, tenderly kissing me and then spanking my bare bottom. "In ten minutes more my maid will come to undress me, and it would never do for her to know that I entertained you in my room." I was scarcely able to rise from her arms after such a long and exhaustive embrace. I was like a squeezed and sucked orange; my vigour was all gone. It was fortunate that my ship was to sail the next day. I was midshipman under my first orders, and I had to go. If the intrigue had been pursued I have no doubt it would have ruined Charlotta's reputation and also my health.'

"And now, Captain, tell us another story," was the persistent cry of all the ladies in concert.

THE CAPTAIN'S THIRD STORY

'After I had grown to manhood I was one summer at a place of public resort in the highlands of Scotland. One night after I had gone to bed I heard voices close beside me; then I noticed that my head lay close to a door which separated my room from the adjoining one. The voices were evidently those of a young married couple in bed, and like myself, close to the door which separated my rooms from theirs. I heard kisses and then a sound as if the lady's buttocks were being spanked; then there was a struggle, and the young man said in a coaxing tone: "Please, dear Alice, do let me."

'"No, Charlie," she replied, "you ought to be ashamed of yourself; I am right in the midst of my period, and I have been bleeding all day; wait till you come next week and you shall have some; and be sure to bring some condrums with you; there is none left, and it would be dreadful to make a baby so soon. Now lie on your side of the bed and sleep. Don't squeeze my thighs that way; it only makes you worse." The sweet voice of Alice now began to grow angry; I heard Charlie turn over and they soon went to sleep.

'My passions were aroused and my shaft grew as big as my thumb, but I lay perfectly quiet during the conversation so as to keep them in ignorance that they had a listener.

'The next morning they were near me at the breakfast

table. Alice was a petite blonde, the smallest and youngest bride I had ever seen in Great Britain. She was so slender and had such large, innocent eyes that she looked like a child in a woman's dress. Charlie was a young surgeon, he was about my own age, and his size and appearance resembled my own.

'After breakfast he started for Edinburgh, where he practised during the week, and returned to his bride to pass the Sunday. During his absence, I paid assiduous attention to Alice, hoping to engage her in an intrigue, but I could make no impression on her whatever. She was a lively little thing, but her life was all for Charlie, with whom I could see she was dead in love. I longed to possess her, if only one embrace; her indifference only made me long for her more madly; all the week I went to bed with a stiff and hot shaft, close to the beauty but unknown to her. Saturday night brought Charlie all radiant with the promise I had overheard Alice give him the week before; I sat in my room reading when at early bedtime they came to their room. The kisses they exchanged when the door was shut were aggravating to me; my shaft became perfectly rigid; just at this moment there came a call for Charlie to go to a neighbouring hamlet and set a broken limb. With a muttered curse he reluctantly obeyed the call; I knew it would take him three hours at least. I listened to Alice undressing, then I heard the tinkle of a little stream of water in crockery, and went to bed. Night after night the little bride had gone to sleep unconscious that she was near me, and now she was asleep again, as I could tell by her regular breathing; but tonight her door was unlocked for Charlie. Would it be possible for me to impersonate him? The risk would be a terrible one, but the rigidity of my shaft put an end to reason, and conscience, if I could fill those graceful little loins of her but once the world might come to an end for all I cared. I stole softly in my shirt and drawers out into the corridor and into Alice's room, I crept into bed with her and took her in my arms. I caressed her cunning round bosoms and felt her plump and polished thighs. They were much larger than I imagined they were when I saw her dressed. She had a few little thin curls between them which I was daintily fingering when she woke up. "So you have come, Charlie," she said. For reply I fastened my mouth to hers and we continued to exchange kisses. She was honestly ready to give Charlie what she promised him, she opened her legs for the expected charge and I did not disappoint her, my crest, entered with delicious tightness. "What a great, clumsy condrum you have on," she said. From this I inferred that my naked shaft was much larger than Charlie's with a condrum on. I gave a plunge that drove my crest in far among the quivering membranes, far up in her loins, I was in rapture, the burning moments repaid me for my longing, nay for all possible retribution to come. She enjoyed it as much as I did, judging from the increased ardour of her kisses and the motion of her thighs. I gave another plunge so deep that my crest seemed to heave her very bosom. "Oh, Charlie!" she exclaimed, with a dying sigh.

'Another plunge, and the sheath of the young bride was

flooded with the mingled gushes; a moment of ineffable satisfaction, of perfect bliss; then she suddenly scrambled from beneath me. "The condrum must have burst," she said, hastily pouring water into the basin and washing away. Pretty soon she came back into bed and nestled in my arms. I pretended to be overcome with drowsiness and languor, and answered two or three of her questions with an inarticulate sound. The completeness with which she melted was soon evident from the deep sleep of exhaustion into which she sank. Then I stole silently from her bed into my own, but did not go to sleep. I waited anxiously for Charlie's return. In due time he came; Alice awoke while he was undressing. "Why did you go out?" I heard her ask him drowsily, meaning why had he got up and gone out after he had gone to bed with her.

"'I had to go," he said meaning he had to answer a profession call. She thought he had a necessary occasion to go into the yard. I heard her yawn and turn over as he got into bed with her, and then the significant sound of the creaking of the bed made me more jealous. This was followed by Charlie's deep sigh; then all was still save for the regular breathing of the two sleepers. It made me happy to hear that Alice had not joined in the sighing. I believe this gave me more pleasure than my successful escape from discovery. The next morning at breakfast Alice looked me right in the face with her large, innocent eyes, perfectly unconscious that but a few hours before she had rapturously melted in my arms.'

As the ladies still clamoured for another tale, I began once more.

THE CAPTAIN'S FOURTH STORY

'During one of my stays in port my uncle, who was a member of the Ministry, needed a confidential messenger to one of the German courts; he offered to send me. I accepted the mission with pleasure; the business took me but a few days, during which time I mingled in the festivities of the court. The sovereign was very gracious to me; his spouse I did not see, although it was said she was in the gallery of the dining hall during one of the state dinners at which I was present. It was known to all when I was to return, and on the evening before I started I had declined several invitations that I might get ready to go. Just at nightfall I received the following singular note:

A lady sends her compliments to Lord Herbert, and begs that he will call at No. 300 R —— Street

'I hesitated as to what to do all the time I was enjoying my after-dinner cigar, but I finally put a pistol in my pocket and proceeded to the place named. It was a neat house in a respectable street. I was received at the door by a nice elderly lady and ushered into a well but plainly furnished room. She thanked me for being so kind as to come. "I have received you at the door myself," she said, "because I thought it best to have my servants away; it is a strange request I have to make to you, but your gallantry is known. May I rely on your honour to keep it secret whether you grant it or not?" I assured her she might. "My foster-daughter, whom I dearly love," she continued, "is married, but the union has not been blessed with children: her husband is very unjust and is making her life wretched, for she loves him; she can endure his reproaches no longer. I have known it was not her fault and I hope I have advised her rightly."

"'Perhaps so," said I, "but what have I to do with it? I leave the city tomorrow probably never to see it again."

"'This is the very reason," she said, "that I have invited you to come here to meet her. She has seen you and wishes her child to inherit your noble blood and handsome person, and this once accomplished never to see or be seen again by you, Sire; it is the desire for an heir, and not wantonness, that has influenced her. Do you consent?"

"'I must see the lady," I replied.

"'She would die of mortification if you should see her and reject her," said the old lady, "but there is no fear of that; if you are pleased with her, go up and kiss her hand when I present you." She then conducted me upstairs and opened a chamber door; a lady was standing in the centre of the room looking timidly at me as I entered. As soon as I saw her I loosened my grasp on the pistol which I had in my pocket; all fear of treachery vanished from my mind, another sentiment immediately took its place. I approached her and kissed her hand; the old lady shut the door and retired. I was alone with a woman not indeed beautiful, but very interesting, her figure was fine, and her features, though irregular, were pleasing. Her eyes fell to the carpet, the ensign of modesty warmed in her cheeks, receded and left them pale, and then showed again more rosy than before. Her hand trembled in mine, her attire made no accession to her appearance, she was dressed in plain muslin without an ornament, her hair was plainly brushed, but there was that in her air which convinced me that she was a lady, and that, too , in an embarrassing position.

"'Fair lady," said I, "your choice has fallen on me, who can appreciate your delicacy, notwithstanding the strange circumstances which force you to do this." A grateful smile lighted up her fine face for an instant, but she involuntarily averted her cheek from the kiss I pressed upon it. She did not reply, nor did she speak once during the whole interview; by this time I felt that the task of getting her with a child would be the most agreeable one that had ever fallen to my lot. She stood passive in a deep reverie, looking almost unconscious while I unfastened her dress and let it fall to the floor; her undergarments were of the finest lawn and lace, and the stud that fastened her chemise was a large diamond, which only confirmed my opinion that she was a lady of high station. I kissed her beautiful white bosoms, which were now disclosed; she awoke from her reverie with another deep blush, and going to the other side of the bed, took off her shoes with her back to me. Then she dropped off her petticoat, got into bed and covered herself up, face and all. I was soon undressed and followed; I took her in my arms and kissed her tenderly; she suffered my lips to revel on her ripe mouth but her lips did not move to return my kisses. My hands wandered over all parts of her fine form. As long as they lingered on her bosoms she was passive, but when I played too wantonly with the curls at her loins, she grew restless. I was excited by her unresisting form beneath me and parted her thighs. My crest entered the Elysian Fields. At least, the promised joys of the Elysian Fields would not have tempted me to withdraw it. It entered where it was surrounded by moist, warm clinging tissues alive with affinity to its sensitive touch. Still she lay passive. I put my arms under the small of her back and holding her firmly, gave a plunge which sent my crest in till it touched her womb. She could no longer restrain from manifesting her delight; she wrapped her arms around me; I gave another thrust which unsealed the fountain of my glands, and then another which planted the gushing sperm in the midst of her loins. She held my face between her hands and gazed and put up her lips for the first and only kiss she had exchanged with me; our lips were glued together till the last drop trickled from my crest and the thrilling rapture slowly faded and left me nearly lifeless in her arms. The life which she had ravished from me could hardly fail to quicken her womb, and her melting gaze as she received it would surely stamp that life with my features. We lay perfectly still for a long time, and then the door opened and the old lady called me. I got up to see what she wanted.

'"You will undo what I hope you have done if you stay longer," she said in a whisper. "I do not wish to startle you, but there is danger of discovery. Lie perfectly still on your back darling," she added to the lady in bed, "and it will be a fine boy." I dressed and stepped to the bedside; the sheet was drawn and her forehead alone was visible. I kissed it and withdrew.

'The old lady soon followed me and put a ring into my hand as she dismissed me hastily from the door. "She begs you to accept it in token of her admiration and respect." she said. "Her love is all for her husband." I should not have taken it if I had seen, as I did on reaching the hotel, that it was a diamond worth hundreds, on the inside of the ring was engraved the words "In Honour". As had been announced I left the city on the first train. Before proceeding far we met with an accident; no one was injured but we would have to wait for the afternoon train. I got a carriage and rode back to the city, rather than wait there for hours. As I approached the main street I could not cross; we had to wait, as the retinue of the sovereign was passing. By his side sat his august spouse. It was the lady with whom I had lain the night before. She supposed me far on my journey, or she would not have left the seclusion of her palace. She rode unconscious of the presence of the man whose seed was even then germinating in her womb. It is six months since then; the newspapers which we received at port a few days ago announce that there is great rejoicing in a certain capital city. The august spouse is in an interesting condition.'

'You see what you must expect, Inez,' said Anna; 'you and I and Myrzella. What will the black-eyed Pasha say if three blue-eyed babies are born the same night in the harem?' The ladies laughed and then teased for another story. :

'One of you must tell it, then,' said I. When they found out that I would tell no more, inquiries were made for the scarf.

Virginia produced it and threw it to a lady whom she named Eli Jelis, from Arabia. She, like Anna, was tall and slender, but there all resemblance between them ceased. The Arab girl had hair and eyes as black as jet and skin like the colour of rich cream. She took the scarf and shook it out to its full length, displaying the spot were Zuleika's blood had stained it. 'You will excuse me if I give you a dance instead of a story,' she said, springing lightly to her feet and waving the long thin fabric high over her head. She accompanied the waving motion with the most beautiful dancing I ever saw. Her slender but finely-rounded limbs seemed to float through the air, her feet came to the carpet with a touch too light to crush a rose leaf; her shining black hair was unbound and reached her ankles, it floated from side to side like a cloud as she danced, her motion, without losing its grace, became more rapid, the colour came to her cheeks, her large lustrous black eyes flashed under the dark lashes. Still the dance became more rapid, her round bosoms did not quiver; at last her whole form seemed to float in the air. Then one toe lightly touched the carpet and the other pointed to the ceiling directly over her head; for an instant between her widely opened thighs, was disclosed a long crimson gash amid the parted curls. In another instant she was standing upright and motionless before me; her hands were folded on her bosom and her head bowed in oriental submission; her hair slowly ceased to wave and fell to her ankles in a veil. 'It was very graceful, my charming Eli Jelis,' said I, 'but I cannot let you off from your story.'

'My story is some of it so disgraceful that I cannot look you in the face and tell it,' she replied, and turning with her back towards me, the beautiful girl told the following tale.

THE ARABIAN LADY'S STORY

"'I was born in the dominions of the Imium of Yemen. When I was fifteen years old I was selected by one of his agents for his harem. My parents were well pleased with my preferment, and I set out from home with girlish glee. On being introduced to the harem, I was bathed and elegantly dressed, then I was led to a room where the Imium was sitting conversing with the ladies. He was an old man with a countenance indicating a feeble character. The conversation showed the supremacy which was exercised over him by his wife, Ayessha, a very fat lady whose corpulence seemed her only charm. After a while the Imium began to look at me a great deal, which I could see she noticed. At last he called me to his side, where I stood with his bare arm around my waist answering questions. His arm gradually lowered and I felt his hand under my petticoats. I supposed he thought the other ladies did not see him, for I was standing close to his side; the eyes of Ayessha, however, were on the alert; they flashed with anger. The Imium's hand explored my thighs and at last his finger entered a place where no man had ever before touched. It felt its way carefully in and soon met with an obstruction; the pressure upon, though slight was very disagreeable to me, but I was afraid to repulse him. What I did not dare to do, Ayessha did. "Your highness," she said, "has promised to present a virgin to the Imium of Muscat. I think this one will do in default of a better one."

"'Yes, she is a virgin," he replied, partly answering her and partly giving vent to his own thoughts.

"'Shall I order the chief eunuch to see to her?" Ayessha asked. The Imium gave a long look at me, then he looked at the black thunder cloud on the brow of Ayessha, from beneath which her beadlike eyes were flashing. He then took his hands away from me with a sigh.

"'Yes," said he, "you may give the order." I suppose she was in possession of some state secret which controlled him or it may have been her graceful charms which rewarded his obedience. The next day I was on the road to Muscat, where, after several days journey, was duly presented. The Imium received his present gracefully, I heard him say a bale of rich goods should be returned to my former lord, then he ordered the female slaves to care for me tenderly. They bathed me and perfumed me and dressed me in the richest apparel and jewellery, then they led me to a sumptuous repast; they could not do too much for me, whom their lord delighted to honour. After super the Imium came into the women's apartments. I had learned from the slave girls that Fatima was his favourite wife. She was a beautiful woman, but I found afterwards that she had a cruel pitiless heart. She did not seem to care for the attentions her lord lavished on me; I even thought there was a gleam of satisfaction on her countenance as he led me to a remote part of the harem. We passed through two or three doors until nothing could be heard of the sounds of music or conversation we had just left. We were now in a rich apartment with an elegant bed in it; as I was somewhat agitated, the Imium sat down on a sofa beside me and began to enjoy his conversation. I knew what was coming, but I neither desired nor dreaded it much. "Now please undress yourself," he said. I obeyed at once, taking off everything but my chemise; in the meantime he stripped stark naked. It made my heart beat violently as I looked for the first time on a man's shaft ready for action. He came and unbuttoned my chemise and let it fall to the floor. I covered my face with my hands. He lifted me and laid me on my back on the bed close to the edge of it, and kneeled on the floor beside me. Then he spread my thighs wide apart, opened the lips between them and made a critical examination of my virginity. "By Allah," he cried, "a crescent-shaped maiden-head; it brings luck to the captor."

"'I am glad it pleases you, my lord," I cried timidly. At this moment he gave a sudden cry of agony and fell across me. I took my hands from my face and saw Fatima holding a shawl tightly around his head while a man I had never seen before was driving a dagger into his body with repeated blows. I tried to call out, but my voice was frozen with horror.

"'Dare to make a noise," said Fatima, "and you shall share his fate." I knelt to plead for my life, but they took no further notice of me till they had satisfied themselves

that the Imium was dead. Fatima flung the covers over
the body. "Let me be the first to congratulate you as
Imium of Muscat," she said, turning to her companion.

"'The most beautiful woman in Muscat has the right
to congratulate me," he replied.

'Then he turned toward me and let his eyes rove over
my naked form as he addressed some soothing words to
me. "Have the decency to put on your clothes and
follow me, hussy," said Fatima. While I was dressing, the
Imium parted from Fatima, after giving her some
instructions about the harem to carry out while he went
to confirm his authority with the troops. The
conspiracy, at the crowning act of which I was present,
was perfectly successful, and the new Imium reigned
without opposition. Fatima was absolute in the harem;
she kept me as much as possible out of sight of the new
ruler, though she allowed him to have free access to the
other women. He took every opportunity to speak to
me, but I avoided him with horror. I could not forget the
scene of the assassination. One evening, after he had
been more persistent in his intentions, Fatima called me
into a room alone; she told me to lie down on the bed,
and when I had obeyed her she turned my petticoat up
over my head; I was so afraid of the beautiful tigress, I
dared not stir; I only begged for mercy.

"'Lie still and I shall not hurt you," she said, and,
having pulled my thighs apart, she opened my sheath
with her fingers; I heard the click of scissors and felt a
slight but keen pain; I put my hand involuntarily to the
place and felt that my maiden-head was gone. "Now,"

she remarked, you will not play your arts on the Imium any more on the pretence of being a virgin," I burst into tears of mortification and anger, and went into my room with the blood trickling down my thighs. The next evening when the Imium came into the women's apartment, Fatima hastily ordered me from the room on some errand.

"'Don't be too harsh with the poor maid," he said.

"'Maid," she retorted, contemptuously, "she has lain with half the young men in Yemen!"

"'I will match you a wager on that," he replied. "Very well," she replied, "if you are right you shall lie with her tonight; if I am right I will dispose of her." This conversation was carried on in a low tone, but I overheard it. She arose and bade me follow her the Imium came after us to the bedroom. "Now feel of the hussy," she said, "and satisfy yourself." The Imium, brute as he was, was very much embarrassed, but he drew me to him, put his hand under my clothes and with his finger satisfied himself that my maiden-head was gone. I was then dismissed with my cheeks flaming with rage and shame, and the two devils passed the night together. Once more after this the Imium sought the opportunity to be alone with me, which was baffling.

'Fatima's keen eyes detected him and my fate was sealed. That evening I was seized in my room by the eunuchs, bound and gagged and sewed in a sack; after being carried a short distance in silence the rattling of a boat and the rippling of water revealed to me the awful doom to which I was to be consigned. I could not move;

I could not call, I was lifted and flung into the water and heard the boat row away. I settled slowly down under the waves as my clothes became saturated. The water reached my nostrils; I made in helpless agony a prayer to Allah. As if in answer to it I heard the stroke of oars. They became louder and louder till the water settled over me and I knew no more. I returned to consciousness lying in the bottom of a boat, the sweet moonlight streaming in my face and the eyes of a handsome young man gazing earnestly into my own; he must have been pleased with what he saw there.

"'Sweet hours of paradise, she lives!" he exclaimed, in a tender, manly tone. His attentions were unremitting until I was fully restored and my lungs free of water, then he arranged me in the bottom of his boat with his coat for a pillow. "Lie close," he said, "we may be observed." Then he rowed silently to a place in the suburbs of the city, where he had a little dwelling and made me welcome. He offered me in the most delicate manner some clothing of his own until mine could be dried; then he cooked me a nice meal, and after I was thus refreshed we conversed without reserve. He listened to my story with his face beaming compassion; it lighted with joy when I allowed him to infer that my person as well as my heart was still to be disposed of as far as any man was concerned. I emphasised man, for I thought of the fiendish and jealous rape Fatima had accomplished. Hassan, for that was his name, soon told his story. He had come into the city to seek his fortune, and had been driven to smuggling to obtain a livelihood; it was while on the alert at his vocation that he had saved me. "We must fly before morning," he said, "if we would be safe. I will be the happiest man in the world if you will suffer me to take you to my desert home." So much kindness after so much cruelty completely won my heart; he read my assent in my eyes and, kissing me tenderly, went to make his preparations to go. We were soon both mounted on a single horse and far away from Muscat. We had been an hour on the road and were still borne along at the same unflagging gallop. Hassan held me in front of him like a baby in his arms, often kissing me; his kisses constantly grew more ardent and then I felt his stiff shaft pressing against my person. He suggested that I ride astride for a and I obeyed, turning with my face towards him, and putting my arms around his neck, while my thighs were spread wide over his own. He let the bridle drop over the horse's neck, whose headlong pace subsided into a gentle canter which was like the rocking of a cradle. Hassan put his arm around my loins and lifted me a little; his other hand was busy clearing away the petticoats; then I felt the crest of his naked shaft knocking for entrance between my naked thighs. I was willing to yield to Hassan anything that he wished, but no sooner had the lips of my sheath been penetrated than I involuntarily clung more tightly around his neck, and sustaining myself that way, prevented him from entering further. I found the sensation entirely different, however, from that which I had experienced when the fingers of the Imium had explored the same entrance; Hassan's organ seemed adapted to the place and excited a feeling of pleasure. I offered my mouth to Hassan and returned his passionate kisses with ardour equally warm; a desire to secure more of the delightful intruder overcame my dread of the intrusion; I loosened my hand from Hassan's neck, my weight drove his shaft so completely home, notwithstanding the tightness of the fit, that his crest rested on my womb. I felt so unexpectedly good as it went in that I gave a murmur of delight. The motion of the horse kept partially withdrawing it and then sending it completely in again at every canter. The first thrust – good as it was, being entirely eclipsed by each succeeding one. I could have murmured still louder with delight, but kept quiet for very shame. What would Hassan think of a girl so wanton? But he was in no condition to think, he was fiercely squeezing and kissing me, while at every undulating movement of the cantering horse he seemed to penetrate me farther, and my womb was deeply stirred. It culminated in a melting thrill, and my moisture mingled with the sperm that gushed from Hassan's crest. He reeled in the saddle, but recovered himself. The cantering motion drove his shaft less deeply in as it became more limber. It finally dropped out of me, a limp little thing drowned in the descending moisture. What a conquest for a slender girl to achieve over such a formidable object, I thought, exhausted but triumphant, I laid my head on Hassan's shoulder. "Poor girl," he said, "how it makes you bleed."

"'Never mind," I whispered, and he always remained under the innocent delusion that he got my maiden-head, for the trying scene of that eventful night brought on my periods prematurely, and before morning my petticoats were stained with blood. Twice more during the night he slackened the speed of the horse, and each time we completed an embrace equally satisfactory. At dawn we were beyond the reach of pursuit, safe and free.

Hassan joined his band of wandering Bedouins; the free, wild life just suited me, and I often joined him in his roving expedition. One day, while we were camped in an oasis in the desert, we discovered some travellers a great way off; they had seen our horses and were avoiding us. Our party mounted to pursue and, being the only woman, I was left alone in camp. I watched the chase until they disappeared over a swell in the sand a great many miles away; they, of course would walk their horses back and I could not expect their return for hours, but this gave no concern. No one could approach the spot without being seen, and before they could reach it Mohamed would have carried me safely away. Mohamed was my favourite stallion; he was swifter than the wind, and so gentle he obeyed my slightest wish; he was of a bright wine colour and his shape was perfect, his head was small and gracefully set on his arching neck. His large brown eyes had almost human intelligence. His limbs were slender and he walked so proudly that he seemed to spurn the ground. He came up to me after I was alone, and, after I had fed him from my hand, I spent some time braiding his mane. Then for the want of something else to do, I thought I would take a bath. It was shaded by palm trees from the sultry heat

which glower on the surrounding sand. After bathing I threw myself at length on the short grass which bordered the pool. I was in no hurry to dress, and stretched myself lazily on my back at full length.

'Mohamed came up and stood over me as if for companionship in our loneliness. I amused myself by making him stand with one of his forefeet on either side on my chest; nothing could have induced him to step on me, not even if a gun had suddenly been fired; but there was nothing to startle him, as we were entirely alone. Pretty soon, as stallions will when standing in perfect repose, his shaft hung dangling out; in spirit of mischief I put up my feet, took it between them and began rubbing it gently; it gradually stiffened and his crest hung down between my thighs and pressed against the lips there. He put his head down and touched my bosoms with his velvety nostrils. I still continued to rub up and down on his shaft with my feet until its presence between my thighs awakened a pleasant sensation; in fact, I became wanton with desire and worked my feet more rapidly up and down his shaft. It suddenly shot out and stretched my sheath to its very greatest tension, penetrated me to my loins. I was ravished with the fierce thrill and the stallion's gushing sperm; it found no room in my distended orifice and spurted out of it again alike a fountain over my belly and legs. Luckily for me, the distance between his loins and mine was sufficient to prevent anything but the end of his shaft from entering. Otherwise I think that it would have been driven through the length of my body and have come out of my mouth. As it was, I scrambled out from beneath him with my lust completely quenched. From my waist to my knees I was dripping with the stallions thick milky sperm. I hastened to wash it off and bathe and cool my startled sheath in the pool. For a long time I had to keep Mohamed away from me with a switch, but did not strike him hard; I could not bear to hurt him for the consequence of my own folly.'

Eli Jelis finished, as she had begun, with her back toward me, while I was leaning back against Myrzella and Virginia. The graceful Arabian was astride of my thighs, partly kneeling on the carpet and partly lying on my loins. She played with my genitals all the time she was telling the story, and my shaft got so stiff that she slipped it into her eager sheath. It was sufficiently excited to enjoy the charming retreat where it was cherished; my pendant was fondled by her tapering fingers and caressed by her soft hair which hung down from her loins. It lay luxuriously quiet, but Eli Jelis had been longing all evening for the connection, and she could not keep still; she made wanton little motions with her loins all the while she was speaking, and at every move the moist warm tissues where my crest was hidden quivered with life and imparted their vitality to me. I could have summoned energy to give the thrusts for which she longed, but I postponed it from moment to moment revelling passively in the lascivious situation. Eli Jelis could no longer restrain herself; she finished her story and began to ply her loins up and down my shaft. Though erect to its full size, it was not entirely rigid, and it bent with her vigorous motions. Her position was favourable to the play of her loins, and she moved with greater rapidity. I seemed to have changed my sex and to be a woman actually enjoying the thrusts of her paramour. In a few moments I would have been ripe for melting, but she could not wait; her buttocks settled upon me, her sheath loosened, and her shower flushed my genitals; she sank back, panting, into my arms, which drew my shaft completely out of her and exposed it, like a rising tempest-beater, from the waves; it subsided at once when the stimulating efforts of Eli Jelis were withdrawn. I was not yet ready for another onset; the ladies were too polite to laugh; I had exerted myself too much in their behalf. Eli Jelis threw the scarf and then nestled quietly in my arms. It fell to the ninth lady; she was French and her name was Reneé. The others had done well to leave her until the last, for she was the most beautiful woman in the room. The sweetness and vivacity of her expression, and the grace of her perfect features and her splendid form, made her conspicuous, even in such delightful company.

She was of medium height, with full contour; graceful as a fawn, yet voluptuous in the bold roundness of her bosoms and the grand swell of her thighs; her complexion was wonderfully clear, her snow white skin was so transparent that a delicate pink tinge showed plainly beneath it, especially at the little ears and the small tips of her fingers; the rosy tint was deep on her lips, and her mouth was like an opening red rose; her large hazel eyes were clear and full, and the long lashes that partially veiled them could not conceal their lustre; her hair was a dark chestnut colour, but when the light fell upon it, it was a golden auburn. It curled at the centre of her head, where it was parted, and would have descended in a luxuriant mass to her knees if it had not been carefully confined by combs. The hair at her loins was dark, but had a ruddy tinge. After she had exchanged a kiss with me she reclined in a graceful position at my feet, where I uninterruptedly feasted my eyes on her marvellous beauty while she told her story.

THE FRENCH LADY'S STORY

'When I arrived at the age of sixteen I was still at a convent boarding school in Paris. Lisette, my room mate, was my most intimate friend. I confided to her all my secrets and supposed she did the same to me, especially what we could learn about marriage and sexual intercourse, a subject which has a strange fascination, even for a girl who, like myself, had never engaged in it, but who looked forward to an early marriage with eager anticipation. One evening Lisette came into the room with a triumphant expression; she had something in a small box which she mysteriously produced; it was labelled, *One Superfine Dildo*. She locked the door, and opening the box, revealing a rubber article about the size of a man's shaft ready for action. She explained to me what it was and said she got it from her milliner as a great favour, and had paid fifty francs for it. She was all eagerness to try it. "But Lisette," I said , "If we do, and we ever should get married, our husband would know it."

"'Oh," she replied, "we could easily fool them." Having filled the dildo with warm water, and fastened it around my loins by the strap attached to it, she prevailed upon me to act the man part. She pulled me into bed and seemed perfectly familiar with the proper time to mount her. So far from being hurt by the thing, Lisette seemed to enjoy every moment of it from the time I thrust it into her till she gave a dying sigh and subsided.

'After a while she was ready to perform the same office for me. When she had got it adjusted I felt the warm thing enter a little way with a sensation not unpleasant; then she gave a thrust with all her might which tore away my maiden-head. It pained me so cruelly that I pushed her off of me and burst into tears, while the blood trickled from the wound and down my thigh. I was terribly enraged at Lisette. At last she confessed to me that my brother had taken her maiden-head while she was on a visit to me during vacation. I finally forgave her when she told me this, and then she pictured to me the delight of an embrace after the virgin wound was healed. I bathed it in warm water and then we went to sleep in each other's arms. Every evening for a week I ministered to Lisette's gratification as on the first night. She told me I was all healed by this time, but I had no desire for her to reciprocate the action with me. One evening after we went to our room, Lisette made herself look as much as possible like a man; she put on a round garden hat and gathered her hair up under it; then she slipped off her skirts, still keeping on her jacket and large drawers; when thus arrayed, with the dildo on, she looked so much like a boy that I actually blushed when she put her arms around my waist and began making love; while doing this she undressed me, and, feigning that it was the marriage night, kissed and caressed me and put me to bed. Then she got on me and crushed her bosoms on mine and squeezed my thighs until I became excited with desire. Then, assuring me that it would not hurt, she affected an entrance between my thighs with the dildo. I was delighted to find that the further it went in the better it felt, and the harder she thrust the more I liked it. It needed but little for me to imagine that I was in the arms of a lover. I wrapped my arms tightly around her and gave a loose rein to my passions; a few more thrusts and my wantonness and desire culminated in a strange thrill that satisfied my lascivious longing and left me nerveless in her arms. Of course we repeated these embraces often afterwards as long as we went to school, and our bosoms developed to matronly proportions that were the envy of all the girls. But, after all, one kiss from a lip covered with a moustache will arouse a girl's passion to a pitch that can never be reached in the arms of a woman. Both Lisette and myself were married soon after leaving school, she to a country gentleman and I to an army officer. Lisette had not been married long when I had good reason to suppose that she kept up a liaison with my brother. I wrote to her, hinting at my painful suspicion, and begging her to make a visit, that I might persuade her to break off a connection so dangerous to herself and my brother.

'She replied, saying she could not come just then, but would be glad if I would receive a visit from her unmarried sister, adding that she was a shy, timid girl, and that a trip to Paris would do her good. Her sister

Aimie accordingly came in due time and was cordially welcomed by me, though I had never seen her before. She was a handsome girl, but very modest; her features were large but pleasing, and she was broad-shouldered and tall, though her bosoms seemed to be flat and her thighs small. She wore her hair very short even for the clipper style then prevailing for young ladies. My husband was at this time off with his regiment, and I thought it would be kind to allow Aimie to sleep with me. When we retired she seemed very awkward about it, but finally followed me to bed. I took her in my arms and kissed her affectionately. She returned the kisses and caresses with so much ardour that I wished Louis, my husband, was in her place. He had been absent long enough for my desires to become like tinder, ready to flame up at a spark. So we lay locked tightly in each other's embrace with our lips glue together. I felt something squeeze up against my thigh which could not be Aimie's arm, for both of them were around me. I put my hand down and felt that it was a man's warm throbbing shaft. I gave a scream and pushed my bedfellow violently from me. "You are not Lisette's sister!" was my assured exclamation.

"'True, charming Reneé," he said, "but I am her brother, and no one will ever know of this but her; will you allow Armand to have one sweet kiss like those you have just given Aimie?" He drew me toward him as he spoke, with the fire of passion glowing on his handsome face. I hesitated, but my sheath was still swelling with wanton emotion, and I suffered him unresistingly to

take me in his arms again. This was not the moral
lecture I had prepared for Lisette; desire was coursing
through my veins. I returned Armand's kisses, I opened
my thighs to facilitate the connection; the touch of his
crest, under the hair, was like the taste of some delicious
fruit unexpectedly presented to a thirsty traveller. I took
it more greedily and swallowed it with a sensation much
more pleasurable. I was ashamed of myself; Armand
would think he was not the first who had taken
advantage of my husband's absence; but I could not
help it, my person had been seduced before my consent
was won, it was too late now for virtue to effect a barrier.
I penetrated to the secret and sensitive depths where
wantonness reigned supreme. The strength and rapidity
of Armand's thrusts showed the vigour of seventeen. I
was transported to the seventh heaven, carrying the
amoured boy in my arms. When I finally returned to the
consciousness of earthly things we lay so still that for a
moment there was not a motion in the bed save that
Armand's shaft was slowly sinking from my sheath with
the balmy flow that filled it. Armand's visit was
prolonged for a week, and no suspicion was excited on
the part of my friends or the servants, nor was the
intrigue, known to any one save Lisette, who teased me
without mercy. It was a week of abandonment to
unrestrained wantonness. I would sometimes ask
Armand, when we were in the privacy of our chamber,
to take his male attire from the trunk and put it on; he
then seemed like a slender and effeminate youth, a mere
fair-faced boy entirely different from the amazon he

appeared in girls clothes, but if I rallied him about his effeminacy he would at once proceed to give a most convincing proof of his vile power. No married embrace ever conferred such rapture; fornication which became so insipid when lawful is so delicious when stolen. The lascivious nights were not enough; we retired every afternoon on the pretence of taking a nap; at every embrace his fresh enthusiasm bewitched me where I was melted by his fervent ardour. But dark and sunken circles came around Armand's eyes; his flesh fell rapidly away, and, when at last he tore himself from me to return home, a hectic fever was consuming him. As for me, I grew plump as he grew thin, and my cheeks bloomed with the stolen pleasure. When my husband returned home on leave of absence he had no occasion to reproach me for want of ardour.

'It had, however, begun to grow monotonous, when we received an invitation from Lisette, seconded by her husband, Adolph, to visit their country seat, which we accepted. We sat up late the first evening, there was so much to talk about, besides which the champagne flowed freely. I enjoyed conversing with such an agreeable man as Adolph; it was pleasant to look at him, for he was fat and jolly, the change was agreeable from being continually with my husband, who was thin and earnest. Lisette and I talked on after our husbands had retired. We finished another bottle of wine, which they had merely opened, and we grew very confidential. We proceeded to undress by the stove and carry our clothes upstairs in our hands. Standing in our chemises, we compared our forms; as of old, they were very similar; we pressed our bosoms together and squeezed together the mouths at our loins.

"'Why do we stand here," I asked, "when we can go to bed and get all we want?"

"'Suppose," she answered, "we should make a mistake in going to our rooms and exchange husbands?"

"'They would kill each other and us, too, if they found it out," I replied.

"'But they won't find it out," said Lisette, "if we keep them too busy to speak." I looked at Lisette to see if she had divined my own adulterous thoughts and to see if she was in earnest; she smiled and nodded, and so did I. Wine and wantonness combined to put us up to that mad frolic. We agreed that I should take her clothes and she should take mine in case of necessity of suddenly escaping to our rooms. As she put her hand on the door knob of my husband's room I felt a pang of jealousy, but I let that disappear and entered Adolph's room. He was sleeping quietly; I laid Lisette's clothes on a chair and got into bed with him. I waited for a few moments for the violent beating of my heart to still, and then nestled up close and put my arms around him; I put aside his moustache and kissed him on the lips; still he did not awaken; then I pulled up his shirt, felt his massive thighs and played with his genitals. They grew under my hand, and he awoke and put his arm around me. I returned his kisses and caresses.

"'Why, Lisette," he said, "how good you are tonight." I replied with kisses, then he got upon me and I soon felt his shaft enter me. It was larger than I had been accustomed to, but very soft. It was a dainty morsel to the glutinous lips through which it passed. They closed upon it with the keenest zest. Adolph's ponderous loins settled down on mine till the hair between was matted into one mass and his shaft caressed by every membrane in my sheath; a tribute as profuse as his excitement had been long. His ample person seemed to be dissolving in my loins. Then he sank down upon me, too weak for some moments to roll down my side and relieve me of his great weight. Before he could give another thrust I was overtaken by the melting thrill; Adolph had not yet reached his climax; he gave two or three more lazy thrusts as I subsided. "I was dreaming of Reneé," he said. Exerting all my strength I pushed him from me as jealously as Lisette would have done had she been in my place; then I turned my back on him. He now realised what a foolish confession he made. "Sweet Lisette," he pleaded, "I don't care a straw for Reneé; she is not half so pretty as you." I obdurately shrugged my shoulders. The Lisette I impersonated would not be pacified; he snuggled up to my back and held me struggling in his arms. I could feel his stiff staff pressed against my buttocks; he patted my thighs and fondled my bosoms and kissed the back of my neck, but I would not turn over. He was so excited with his desire from his half finished job that at last he communicated his wantonness to me. I was ready for another onset, so I turned on my back and he mounted fiercely to the charge. Plunge after plunge in rapid succession again

roused all the sensibilities of my sheath. My mouth was buried under his moustache and the kisses kept time to the rapid play, the glow of the friction became more and more intense, spreading from the place of contact in electric waves all over my frame, and the stolen and guilty pleasure culminated in another melting thrill.

'He soon fell asleep, one hand grasping one of my bosoms and one of his heavy thighs on my own. Cautiously I extracted myself and stole from the room, dripping at every step. Lisette was waiting for me with jealousy and impatience depicted on her countenance. "What have you been doing all this time?" she asked.

'"The same as you have, I suppose," I replied, laughing.

'"I have been standing here this hour and a half," she said. "I was sobered up by the danger when I got into Louis' room, and I dared not get into bed with him." I put my hand suddenly up under Lisette's chemise; the hair at her loins was dry; so were the lips it covered; her story was true; for once in my life I got the better of Lisette. We went to our chambers, she almost crying and I almost bursting with laughter.

'During the rest of our visit she watched me narrowly to see that I was not a moment alone with Adolph; she need not have been so suspicious; the curiosity of wantonness was satisfied with regards to him. When we returned to Paris, Louis joined the army. I had now acquired such a taste of variety that I was pleased at the attentions of a young duke. He sought my company on every public occasion; at last he called at my house. He had sent me a magnificent diamond necklace the day before and it was necessary for me to return it if I was unwilling to pursue the intrigue. In expectation of the interview I dressed as attractive as possible, a dress of pink silk, cut low in the neck, displaying my bosoms to advantage. I wore the diamond necklace, the duke saw it with a smile of pleasure and knelt at my feet and kissed my hand, then he arose and our lips met. I consented to meet him later at a safe place of assignation, and if he had taken his leave all would have gone smoothly, but the duke kept kissing me and prolonged the interview. Though my husband was not expected for a day or two, a servant was liable to enter. I rose to have him go, but he still kept his chair. With one arm around my waist he drew me to him and transferred his kisses from my neck to my bosoms. I bent down and kissed his forehead, desire getting control over us; the duke's hand stole under my skirts and explored all the mysteries they hid, then he lifted one of my legs over his lap and I found myself sitting astride of his thighs, clasped in his arms and our lips glued together. We were foolish to risk ourselves there when in a few hours we could safely revel in each other's arms. The duke produced his stiff shaft and I felt it pleading for entrance between my thighs. I half rose to free myself from his arms, but with such feeble purpose that he pulled me down again and I sat directly upon his crest and my weight forced it into me. It filled me with a sensation of such exquisite pleasure that I abandoned myself to my aroused passions. He could not move freely, but my loins undulated to assist him which made my crisis culminate. My ecstasy was prolonged and I had not finished melting when my husband opened the door! I sprang backwards from the duke's arms, and my skirts fell and covered my nakedness. But the duke was in the very act of spending. The sperm jetted from his rampant crest and splashed on the front of my dress. For a single moment my brain whirled with incongruous thoughts, of which one was that my gown was spoiled, and then I darted from the room; I wrapped myself in a long cloak and hood as I fled; as I passed through the lower hall and gained the front door I heard the trampling of feet and the crash of furniture in the parlour above. I was my husband and the duke engaged in a deadly struggle. The outcome I never knew. I reached a railway station just as a train was leaving. I got aboard and in a short time reached Marseilles. Even then I did not feel safe, and I did not breathe freely till I had put the Mediterranean between myself and France.'

CONCLUSION

Reneé concluded; she now expected her reward; it was her turn at last. The loins of eight of these beautiful women had been stirred to the depths by me and they had melted in my embrace. To four of them I had paid tribute in return. The night would be fittingly crowned by a tribute to the loveliest and last. The charming French girl lay on the cushions with Laura's belly for a pillow. She shot a seductive glance at me and opened her graceful tapering legs. I knelt between them and kissed the grand, snow-white thighs close to the thick, ruddy hair that adorned them. I planted another kiss on her belly just over the womb. From the pink nipples of her bosom I sucked voluptuous kisses. Then my lips fastened on her mouth. She wound a soft arm around me as I stretched myself on her lovely form, and with her other hand she guided my crest to the haven it sought, and I pushed my way slowly in. It was deliciously tight and elastic and hot and juicy. I thrust more than once before my shaft completely entered which was no sooner accomplished than I felt Reneé's frame shudder beneath me and become limp and nerveless; her arms relaxed and her sheath grew loose and flooded with moisture. 'Lie still,' she whispered, 'and I shall be able to finish you.' I was in no hurry. I lay luxuriantly upon her with my crest soaking in the innermost recesses of her

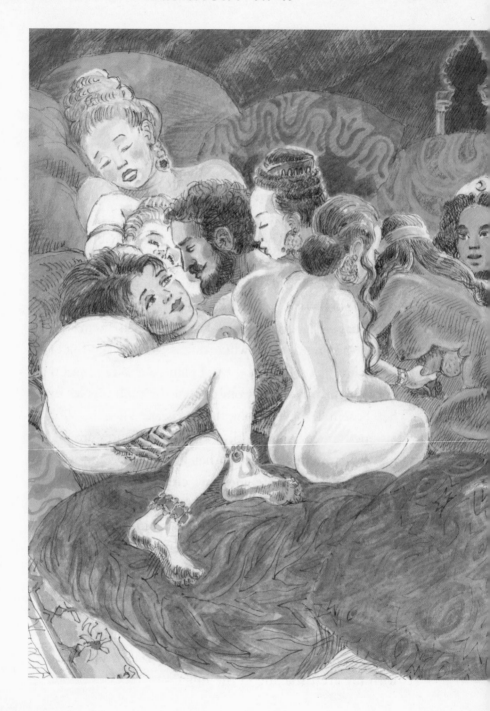

loins. Laura's waist still served her as a pillow, and my lips wandered from Reneé's lips to Laura's fat bosoms, and my fingers searched her equally convenient sheath. Inez nestled up to me and hid the fingers of my other hand deep between her thighs. Helene, on the other side, was fondling my glands. Zuleika, Myrzella and Virginia kissed my back, shoulders and neck. My feet were abandoned to Anna and Eli Jelis, who sat holding them between their thighs with my toes searching their sheaths. The wanton touch of nine charming and amorous women infused me rapidly with some of their own vigour. My shaft became perfectly rigid.

Reneé awoke to the responsibility that rested on her. She darted her tongue into my mouth while I was sucking her lips. Her sheath convulsively contracted and tightly and lasciviously seized my crest. I responded with a deep, prolonged thrust. Then I braced my toes in the hot crevices where they rested and rammed my shaft completely home again and again. Reneé threw her arms around my neck and her legs up over my buttocks and surged her loins up to meet each descending stroke. I felt the crisis approaching. My very marrow seemed to be distilling into my glands. My plunges became more rapid, until the very nerves of my shaft seemed laid bare to the friction. Reneé redoubled her exertions. As her loins rose to meet me she gave them a rotary motion, which made her womb circle around my crest. The supreme moment came at last, and I was completely ravished. My very blood seemed to gush. I gave a groan of ecstasy and sank, almost inanimate, upon the panting form of Reneé. She kept squeezing her sheath to complete her own rapture, and extracted a few more drops. I heard several of the ladies mingle their sighs with her. And my fingers and toes were bathed with their moisture. I lay for a long time unable to stir. 'That will make another blue-eyed boy,' said Myrzella. 'I feel as if I were gotten with twins,' exclaimed Reneé, giving one more squeeze to my diminished shaft.

When I recovered sufficiently to be able to move my first look was at the clock. It was nearly dawn and it was necessary for me to go. The ladies helped me to dress, for I had not the strength of a kitten. Each of them exchanged a tender parting kiss with me, and then I went to the window but I was too weak to climb. I fastened the rope of shawls around under my arms, and all the ladies took hold together and lowered me safely down. I pushed my boat from the shore and set sail. The land breeze was just setting in and I gained the offing, where I descried my ship beating up and down looking for me. In an hour more I was safely on board.

FIN